PILOT & HUXLEY

DAN McGUINESS

graphix

AN IMPRINT OF

SCHOLASTIC

NEW YORK TORONTO LONDON AUCKLAND SYDNEY MEXICO CITY NEW DELHI HONG KONG

TO MY LOVING PARENTS,
ELAINE AND BILL McGUINESS

TEXT AND ILLUSTRATIONS COPYRIGHT © 2011 BY DAN McGUINESS
DESIGN BY DAN McGUINESS AND CLARE OAKES
COVER DESIGN BY PHIL FALCO

FIRST PUBLISHED BY OMNIBUS BOOKS, A DIVISION OF SCHOLASTIC
AUSTRALIA PTY LIMITED, IN 2009.

THIS EDITION PUBLISHED UNDER LICENSE FROM SCHOLASTIC AUSTRALIA PTY LIMITED.

LIBRARY OF CONGRESS CONTROL NUMBER: 2010926309

ISBN 978-0-545-26504-1
10 9 8 7 6 5 4 3 2   11 12 13 14 15
PRINTED IN THE U.S.A.   40
FIRST EDITION, JANUARY 2011

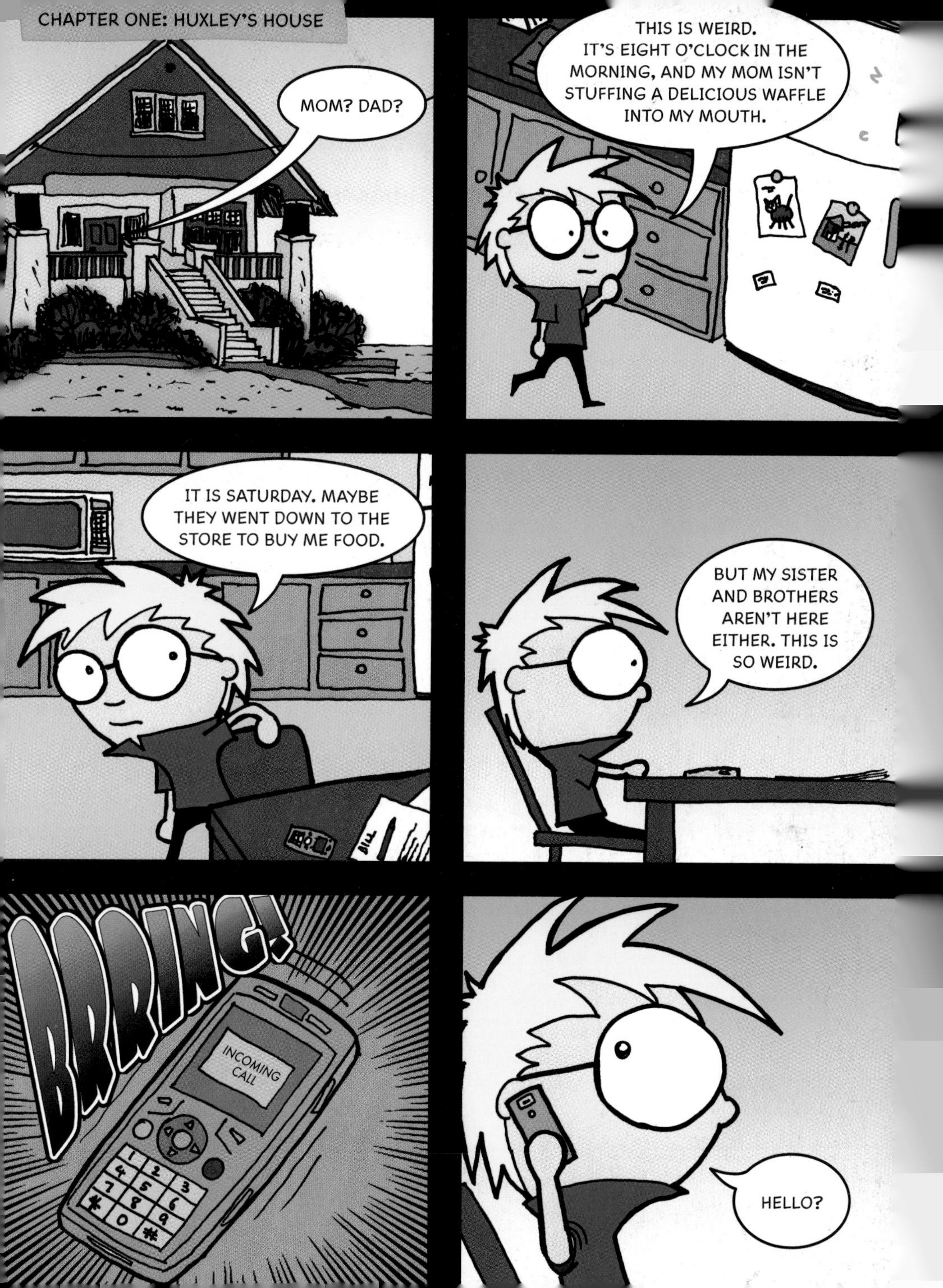
CHAPTER ONE: HUXLEY'S HOUSE
MOM? DAD?
THIS IS WEIRD. IT'S EIGHT O'CLOCK IN THE MORNING, AND MY MOM ISN'T STUFFING A DELICIOUS WAFFLE INTO MY MOUTH.
IT IS SATURDAY. MAYBE THEY WENT DOWN TO THE STORE TO BUY ME FOOD.
BUT MY SISTER AND BROTHERS AREN'T HERE EITHER. THIS IS SO WEIRD.
BRRING!
INCOMING CALL
HELLO?

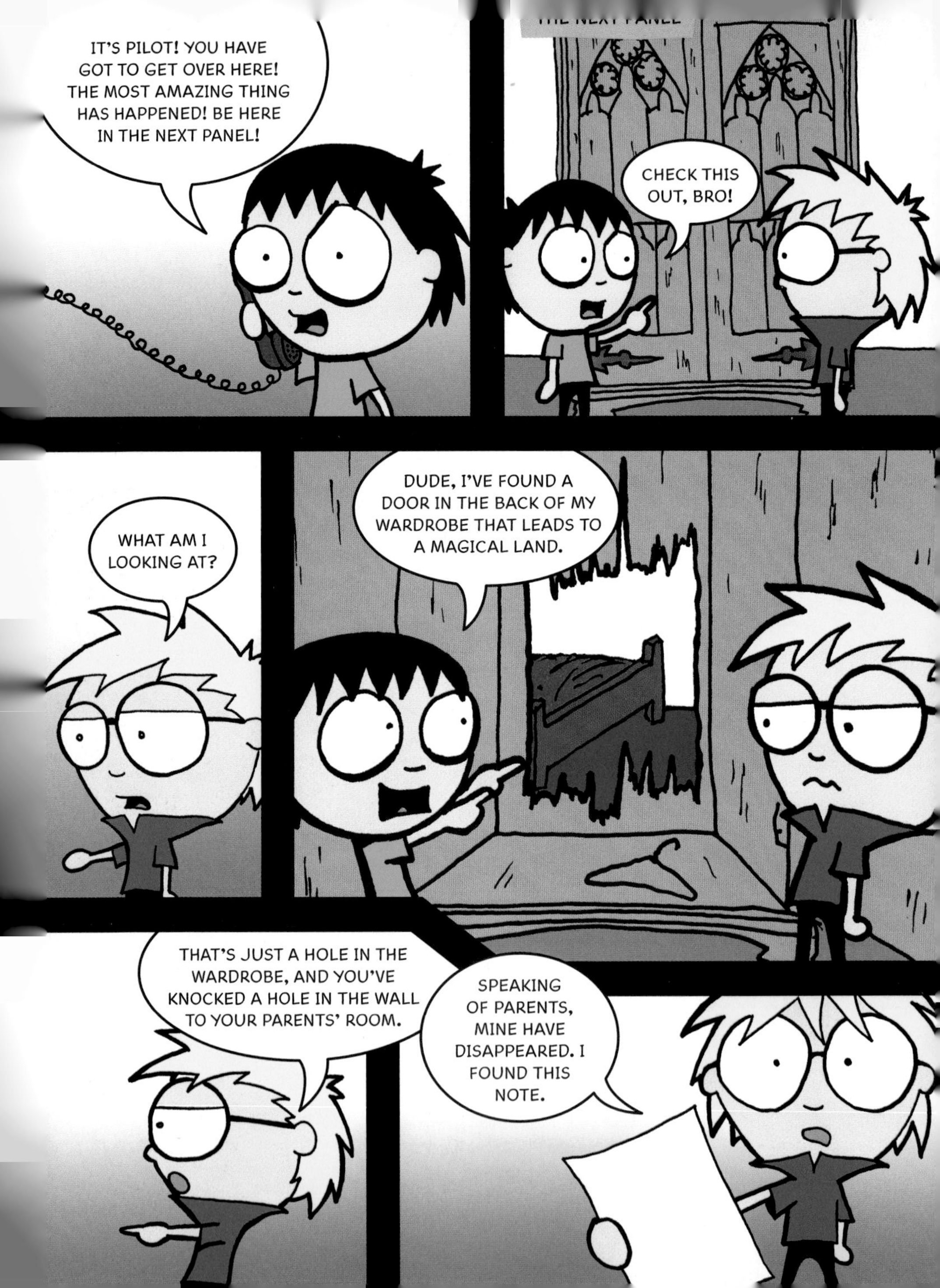
IT'S PILOT! YOU HAVE GOT TO GET OVER HERE! THE MOST AMAZING THING HAS HAPPENED! BE HERE IN THE NEXT PANEL!
CHECK THIS OUT, BRO!
WHAT AM I LOOKING AT?
DUDE, I'VE FOUND A DOOR IN THE BACK OF MY WARDROBE THAT LEADS TO A MAGICAL LAND.
THAT'S JUST A HOLE IN THE WARDROBE, AND YOU'VE KNOCKED A HOLE IN THE WALL TO YOUR PARENTS' ROOM.
SPEAKING OF PARENTS, MINE HAVE DISAPPEARED. I FOUND THIS NOTE.

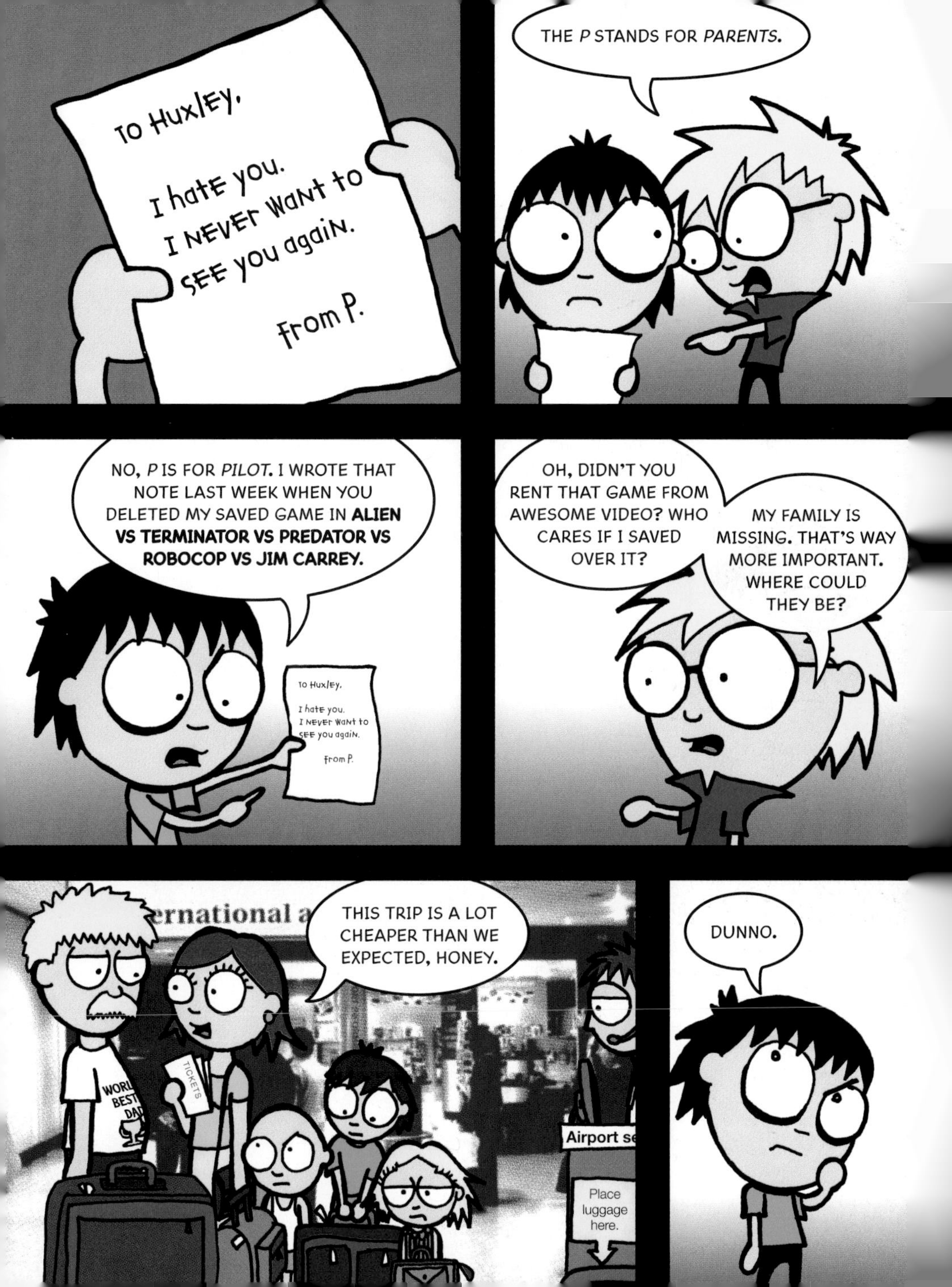
To Huxley,
I hate you.
I never want to
see you again.
From P.
THE P STANDS FOR PARENTS.
NO, P IS FOR PILOT. I WROTE THAT NOTE LAST WEEK WHEN YOU DELETED MY SAVED GAME IN ALIEN VS TERMINATOR VS PREDATOR VS ROBOCOP VS JIM CARREY.
To Huxley, I hate you. I never want to see you again. From P.
OH, DIDN'T YOU RENT THAT GAME FROM AWESOME VIDEO? WHO CARES IF I SAVED OVER IT?
MY FAMILY IS MISSING. THAT'S WAY MORE IMPORTANT. WHERE COULD THEY BE?
THIS TRIP IS A LOT CHEAPER THAN WE EXPECTED, HONEY.
TICKETS
Place luggage here.
DUNNO.

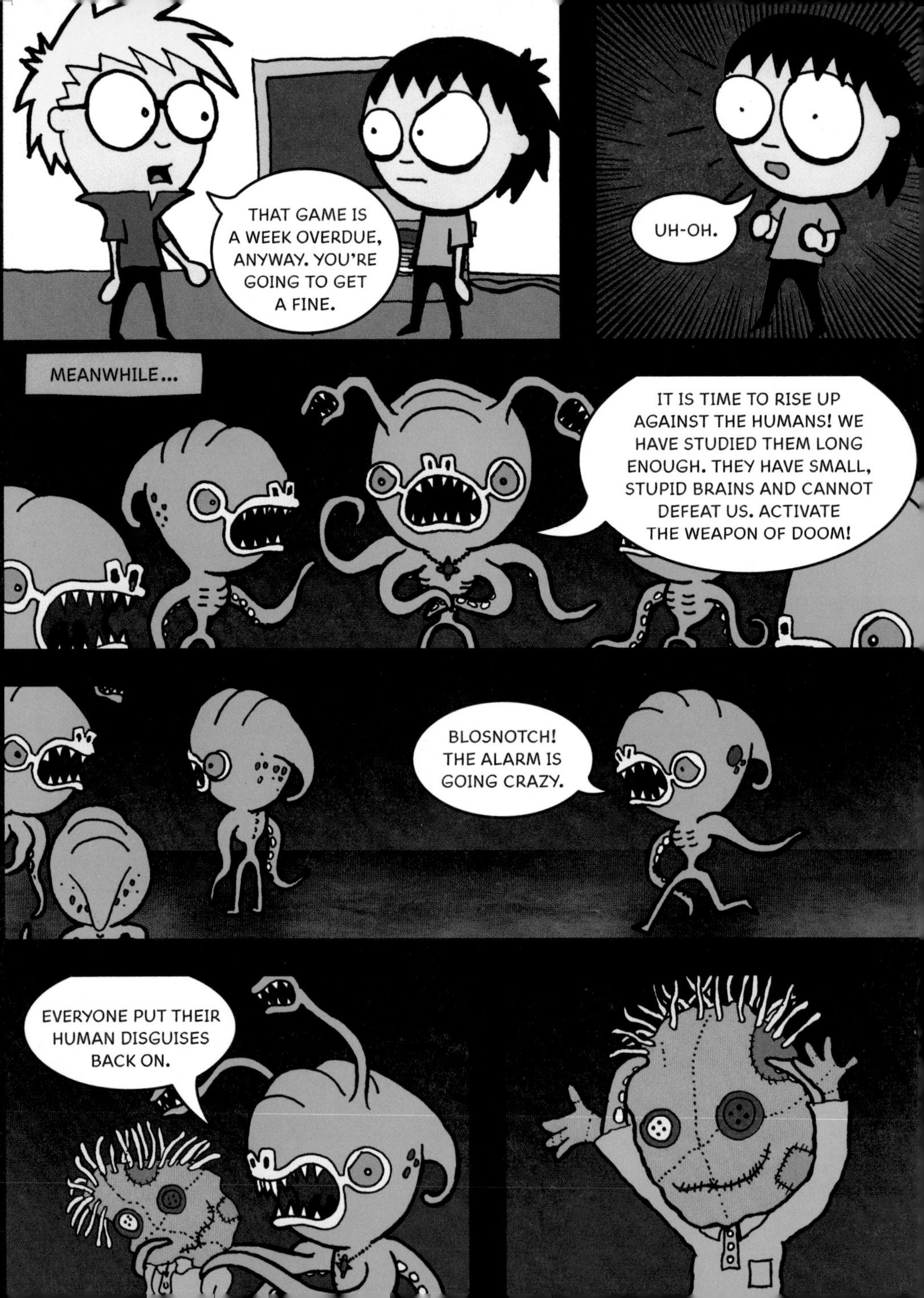
THAT GAME IS A WEEK OVERDUE, ANYWAY. YOU'RE GOING TO GET A FINE.
UH-OH.
MEANWHILE...
IT IS TIME TO RISE UP AGAINST THE HUMANS! WE HAVE STUDIED THEM LONG ENOUGH. THEY HAVE SMALL, STUPID BRAINS AND CANNOT DEFEAT US. ACTIVATE THE WEAPON OF DOOM!
BLOSNOTCH! THE ALARM IS GOING CRAZY.
EVERYONE PUT THEIR HUMAN DISGUISES BACK ON.

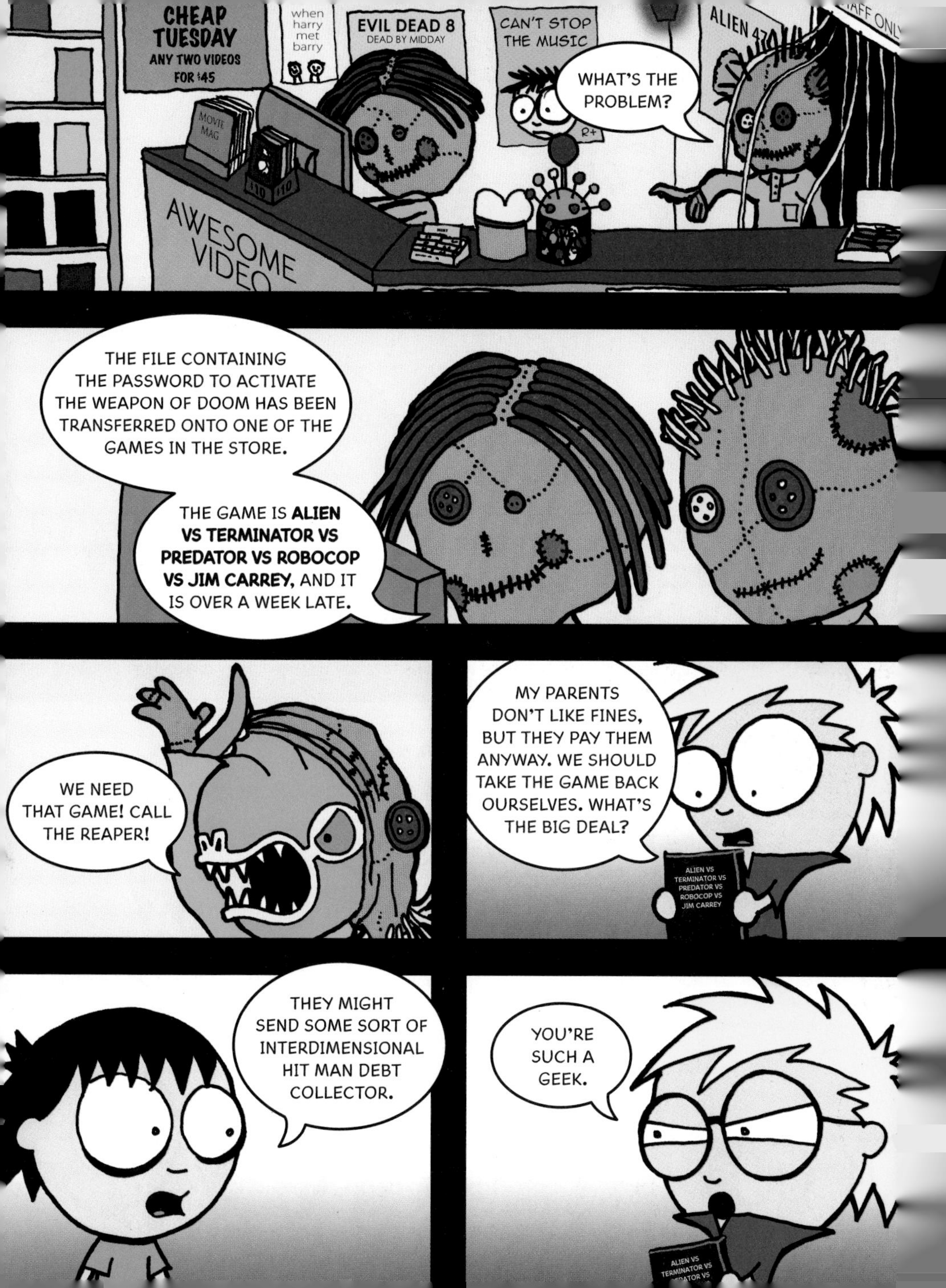
CHEAP TUESDAY
ANY TWO VIDEOS FOR $45
when harry met barry
EVIL DEAD 8
DEAD BY MIDDAY
CAN'T STOP THE MUSIC
R+
ALIEN 47
STAFF ONLY
MOVIE MAG
AWESOME VIDEO
WHAT'S THE PROBLEM?
THE FILE CONTAINING THE PASSWORD TO ACTIVATE THE WEAPON OF DOOM HAS BEEN TRANSFERRED ONTO ONE OF THE GAMES IN THE STORE.
THE GAME IS ALIEN VS TERMINATOR VS PREDATOR VS ROBOCOP VS JIM CARREY, AND IT IS OVER A WEEK LATE.
WE NEED THAT GAME! CALL THE REAPER!
MY PARENTS DON'T LIKE FINES, BUT THEY PAY THEM ANYWAY. WE SHOULD TAKE THE GAME BACK OURSELVES. WHAT'S THE BIG DEAL?
ALIEN VS TERMINATOR VS PREDATOR VS ROBOCOP VS JIM CARREY
THEY MIGHT SEND SOME SORT OF INTERDIMENSIONAL HIT MAN DEBT COLLECTOR.
YOU'RE SUCH A GEEK.

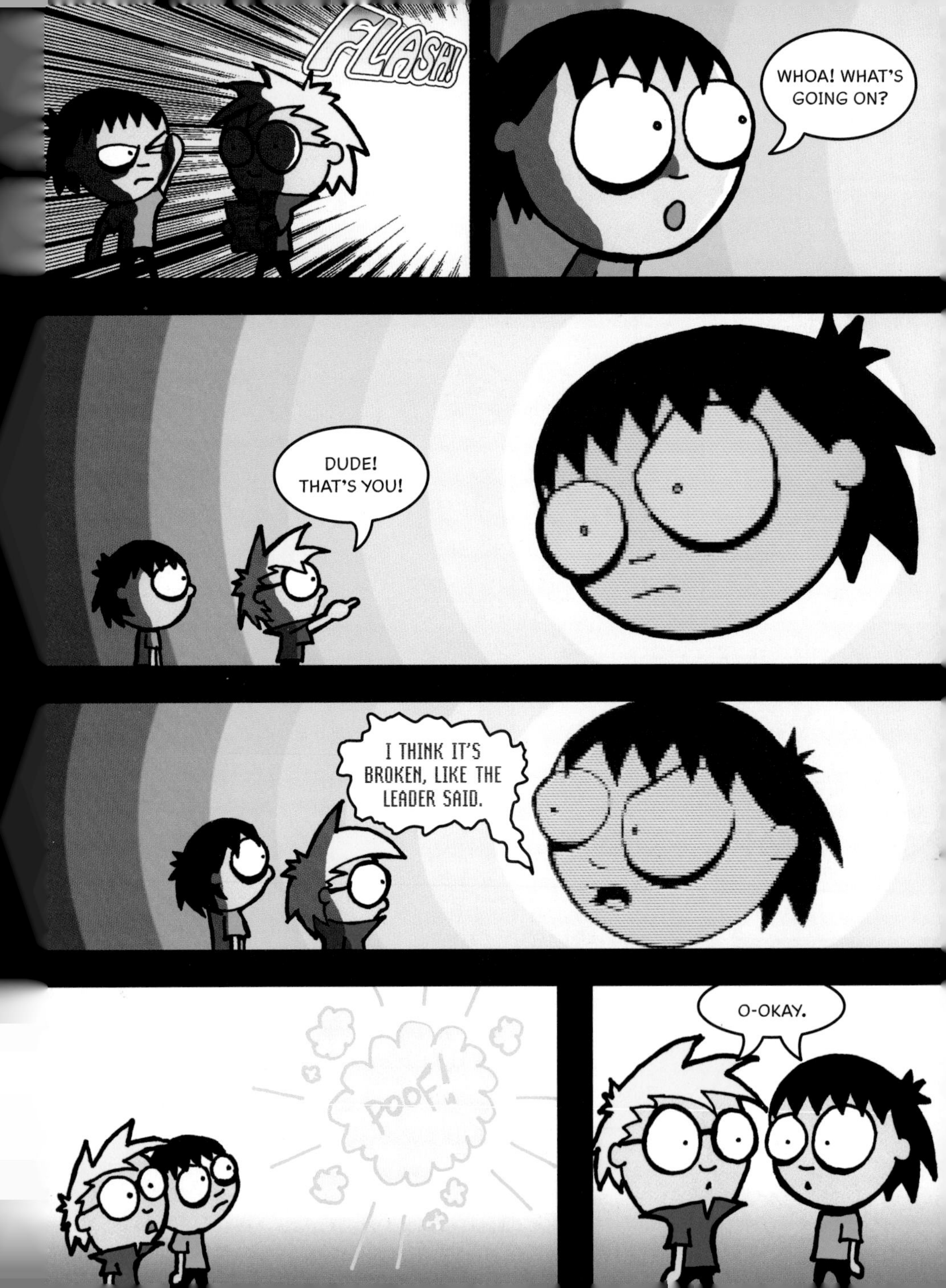
FLASH!
WHOA! WHAT'S GOING ON?
DUDE! THAT'S YOU!
I THINK IT'S BROKEN, LIKE THE LEADER SAID.
POOF!
O-OKAY.

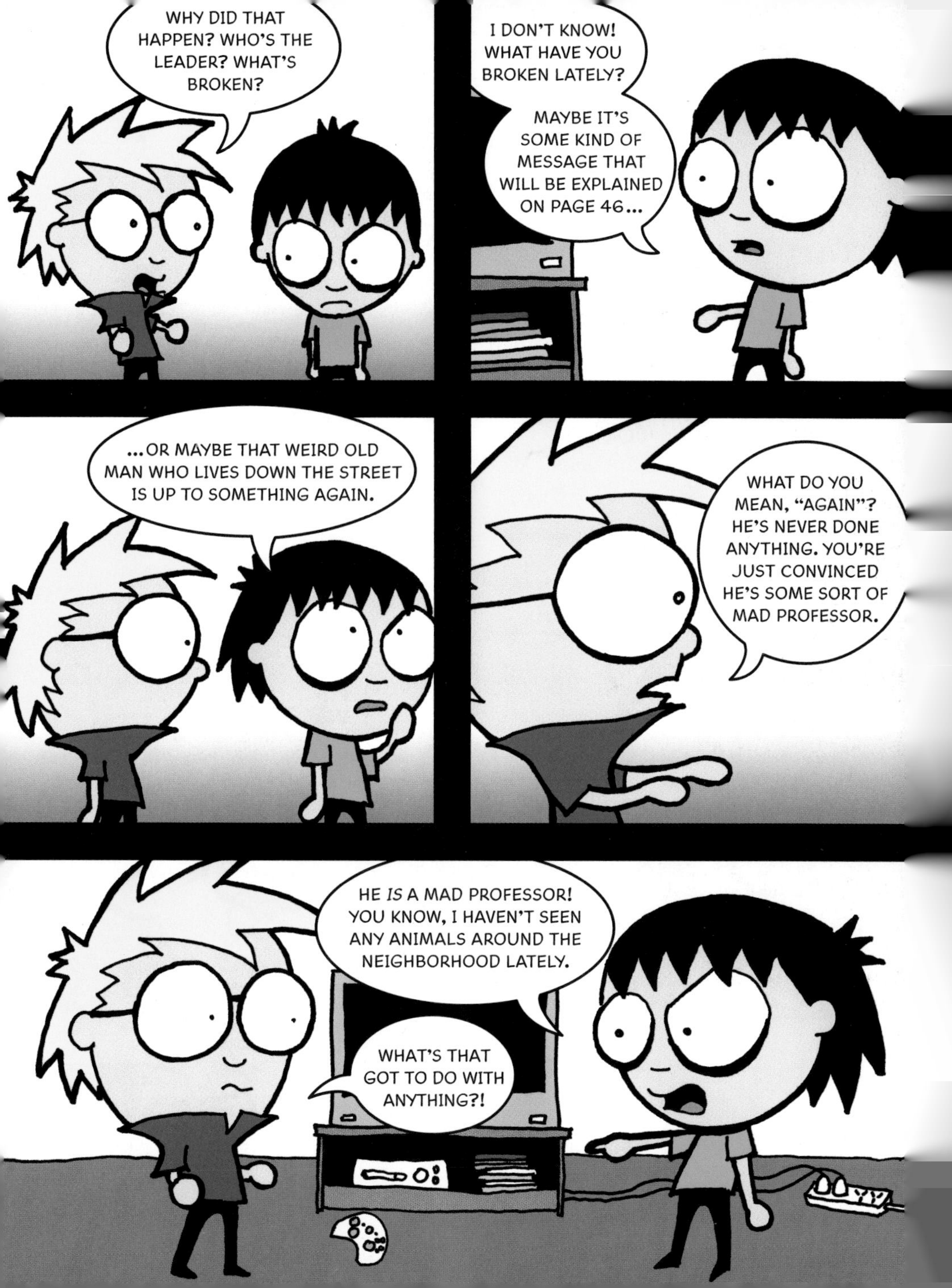
WHY DID THAT HAPPEN? WHO'S THE LEADER? WHAT'S BROKEN?
I DON'T KNOW! WHAT HAVE YOU BROKEN LATELY?
MAYBE IT'S SOME KIND OF MESSAGE THAT WILL BE EXPLAINED ON PAGE 46...
...OR MAYBE THAT WEIRD OLD MAN WHO LIVES DOWN THE STREET IS UP TO SOMETHING AGAIN.
WHAT DO YOU MEAN, "AGAIN"? HE'S NEVER DONE ANYTHING. YOU'RE JUST CONVINCED HE'S SOME SORT OF MAD PROFESSOR.
HE *IS* A MAD PROFESSOR! YOU KNOW, I HAVEN'T SEEN ANY ANIMALS AROUND THE NEIGHBORHOOD LATELY.
WHAT'S THAT GOT TO DO WITH ANYTHING?!

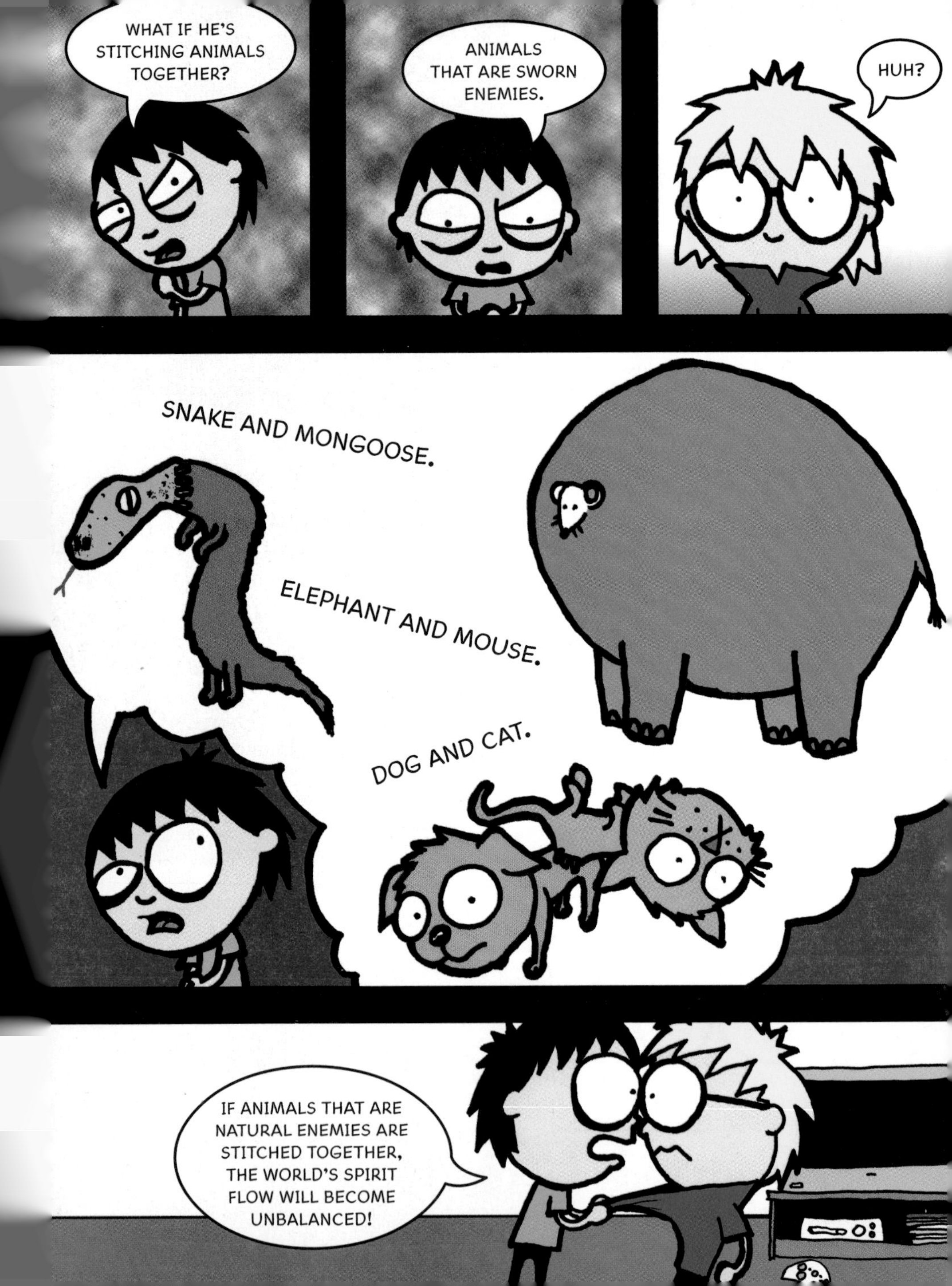
WHAT IF HE'S STITCHING ANIMALS TOGETHER?
ANIMALS THAT ARE SWORN ENEMIES.
HUH?
SNAKE AND MONGOOSE.
ELEPHANT AND MOUSE.
DOG AND CAT.
IF ANIMALS THAT ARE NATURAL ENEMIES ARE STITCHED TOGETHER, THE WORLD'S SPIRIT FLOW WILL BECOME UNBALANCED!

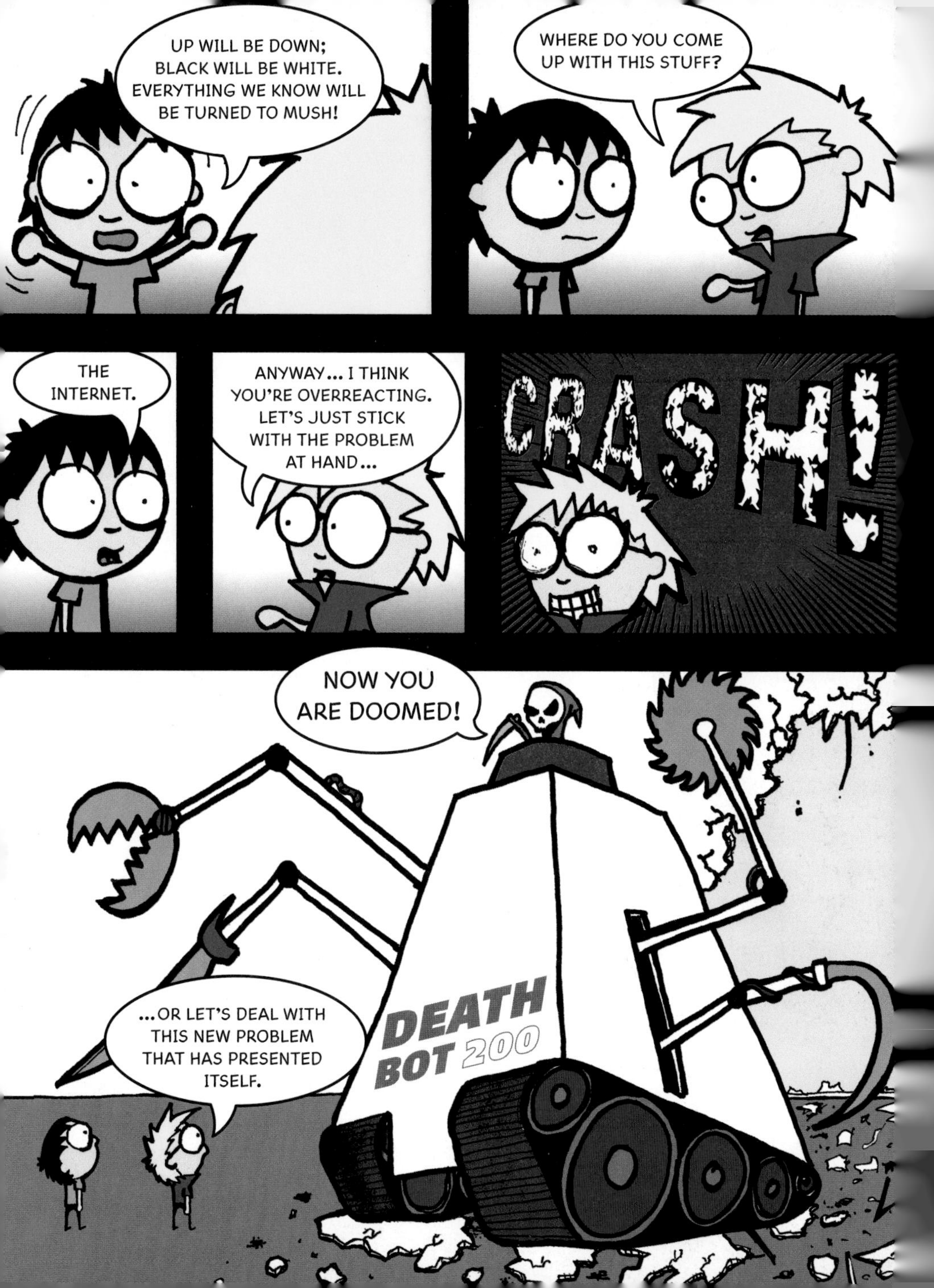
UP WILL BE DOWN; BLACK WILL BE WHITE. EVERYTHING WE KNOW WILL BE TURNED TO MUSH!
WHERE DO YOU COME UP WITH THIS STUFF?
THE INTERNET.
ANYWAY... I THINK YOU'RE OVERREACTING. LET'S JUST STICK WITH THE PROBLEM AT HAND...
CRASH!
NOW YOU ARE DOOMED!
DEATH BOT 200
...OR LET'S DEAL WITH THIS NEW PROBLEM THAT HAS PRESENTED ITSELF.

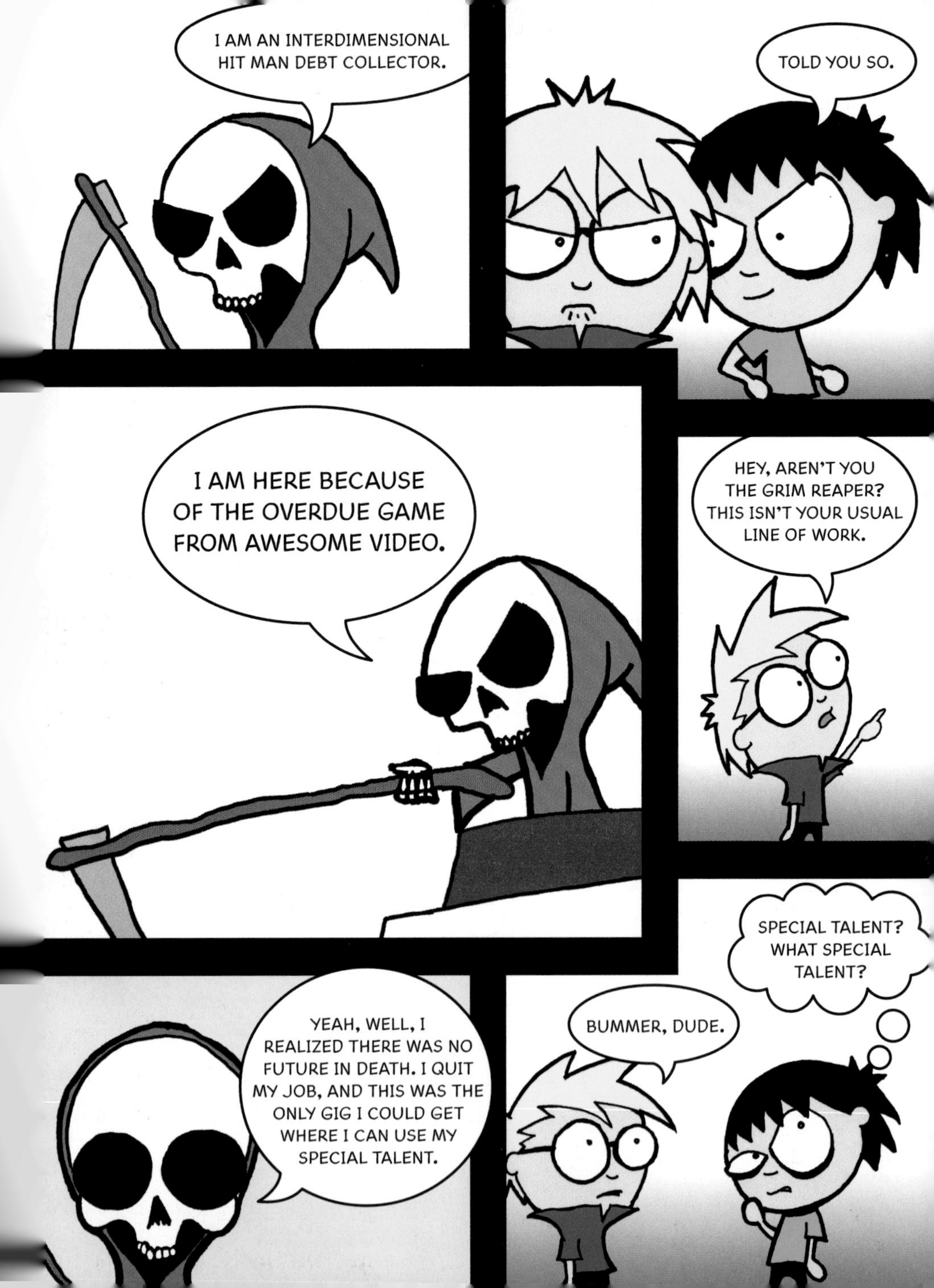
I AM AN INTERDIMENSIONAL HIT MAN DEBT COLLECTOR.
TOLD YOU SO.
I AM HERE BECAUSE OF THE OVERDUE GAME FROM AWESOME VIDEO.
HEY, AREN'T YOU THE GRIM REAPER? THIS ISN'T YOUR USUAL LINE OF WORK.
YEAH, WELL, I REALIZED THERE WAS NO FUTURE IN DEATH. I QUIT MY JOB, AND THIS WAS THE ONLY GIG I COULD GET WHERE I CAN USE MY SPECIAL TALENT.
BUMMER, DUDE.
SPECIAL TALENT? WHAT SPECIAL TALENT?

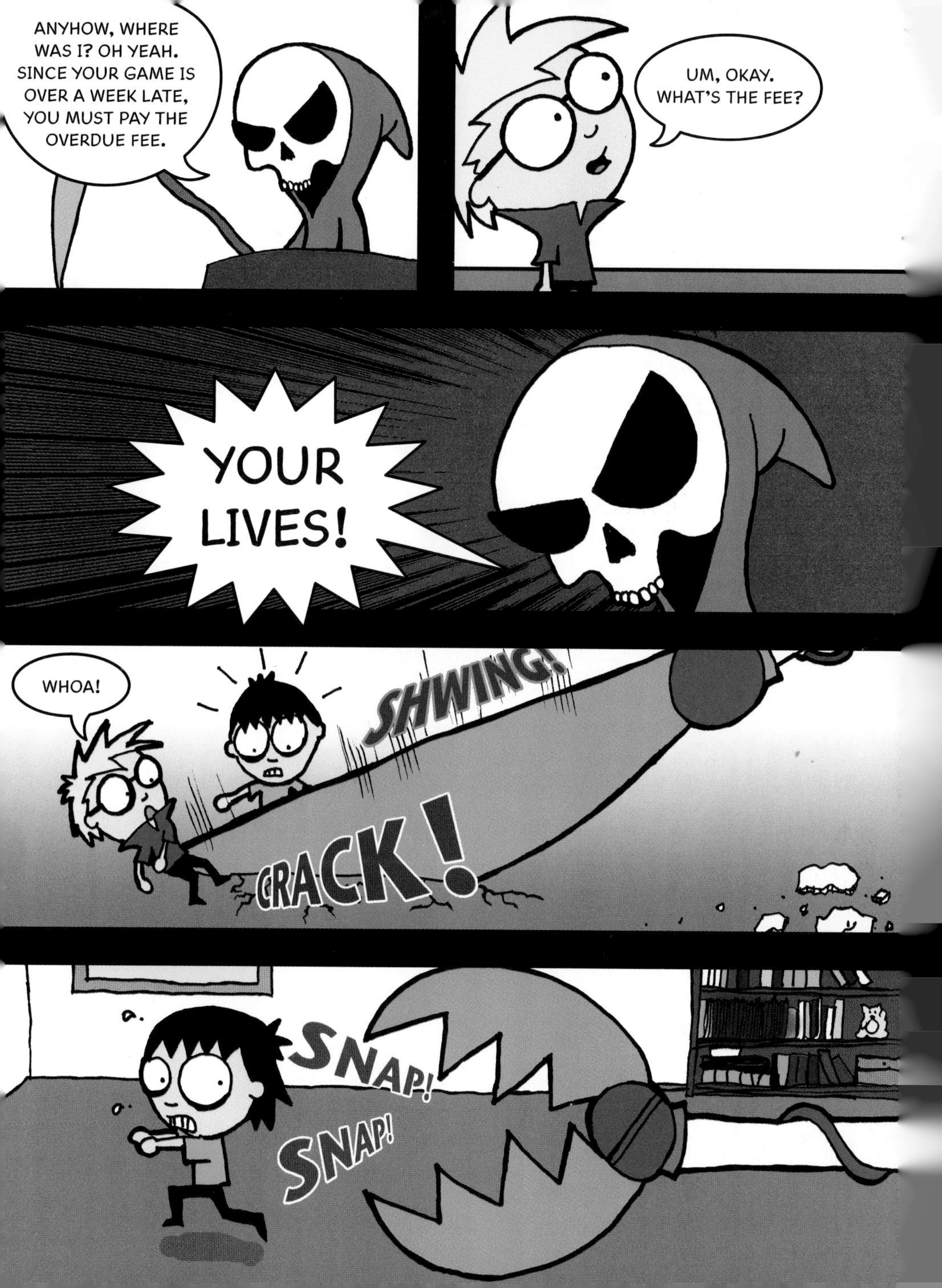

ANYHOW, WHERE WAS I? OH YEAH. SINCE YOUR GAME IS OVER A WEEK LATE, YOU MUST PAY THE OVERDUE FEE.
UM, OKAY. WHAT'S THE FEE?
YOUR LIVES!
WHOA!
SHWING!
CRACK!
SNAP!
SNAP!

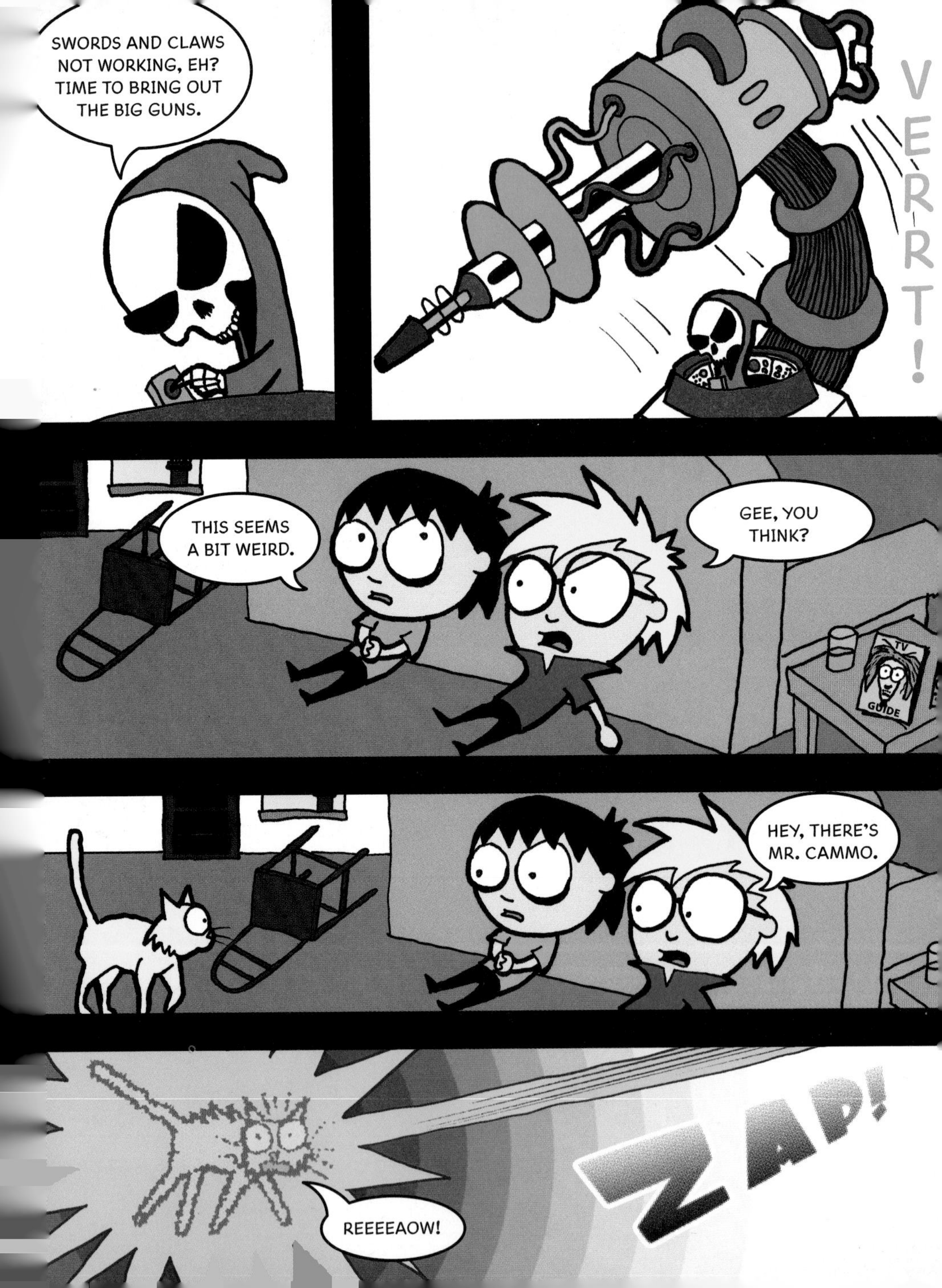
SWORDS AND CLAWS NOT WORKING, EH? TIME TO BRING OUT THE BIG GUNS.
VERRT!
THIS SEEMS A BIT WEIRD.
GEE, YOU THINK?
TV GUIDE
HEY, THERE'S MR. CAMMO.
ZAP!
REEEEAOW!

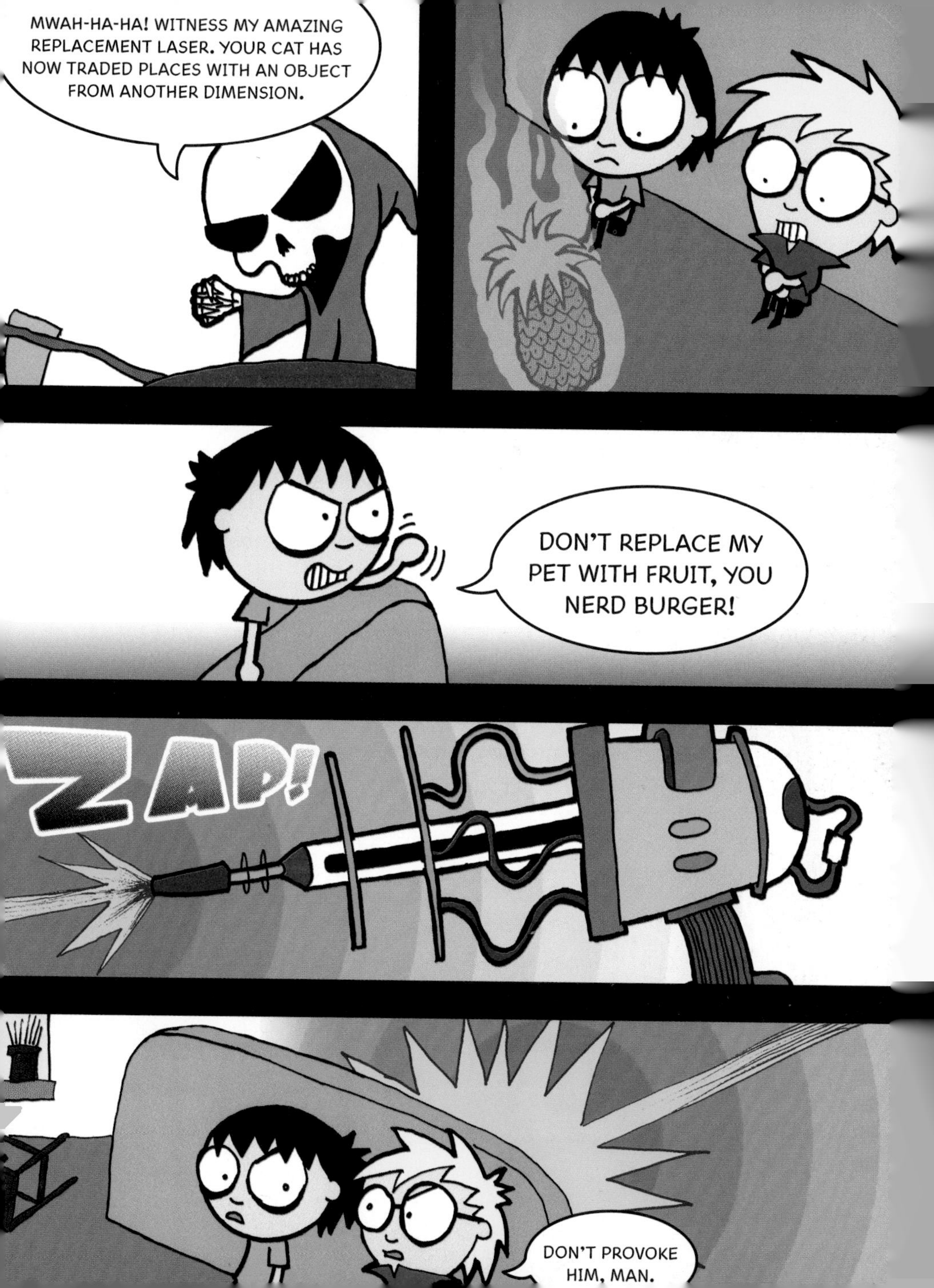
MWAH-HA-HA! WITNESS MY AMAZING REPLACEMENT LASER. YOUR CAT HAS NOW TRADED PLACES WITH AN OBJECT FROM ANOTHER DIMENSION.
DON'T REPLACE MY PET WITH FRUIT, YOU NERD BURGER!
ZAP!
DON'T PROVOKE HIM, MAN.

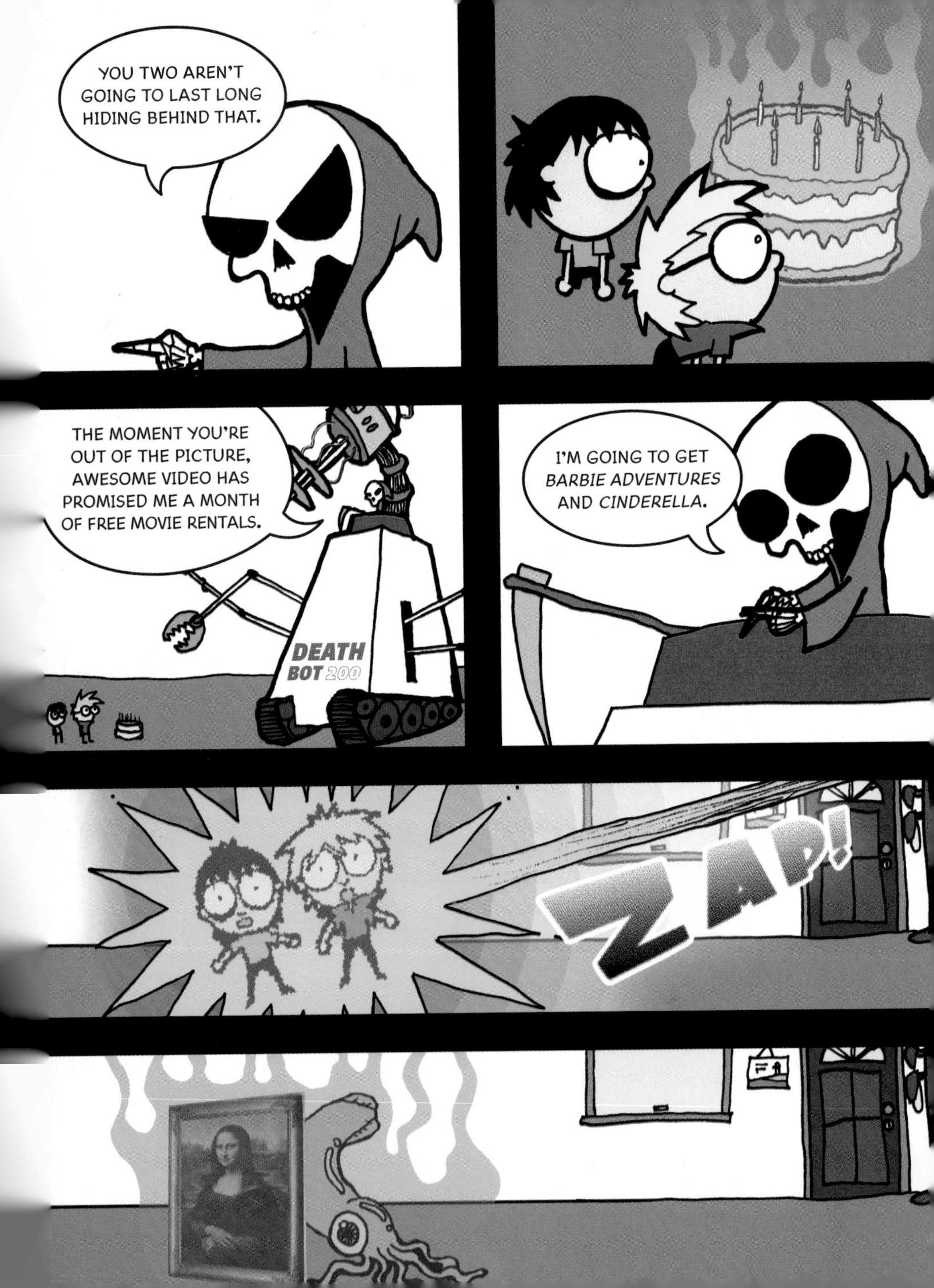
YOU TWO AREN'T GOING TO LAST LONG HIDING BEHIND THAT.
THE MOMENT YOU'RE OUT OF THE PICTURE, AWESOME VIDEO HAS PROMISED ME A MONTH OF FREE MOVIE RENTALS.
DEATH BOT 200
I'M GOING TO GET *BARBIE ADVENTURES* AND *CINDERELLA*.
ZAP!

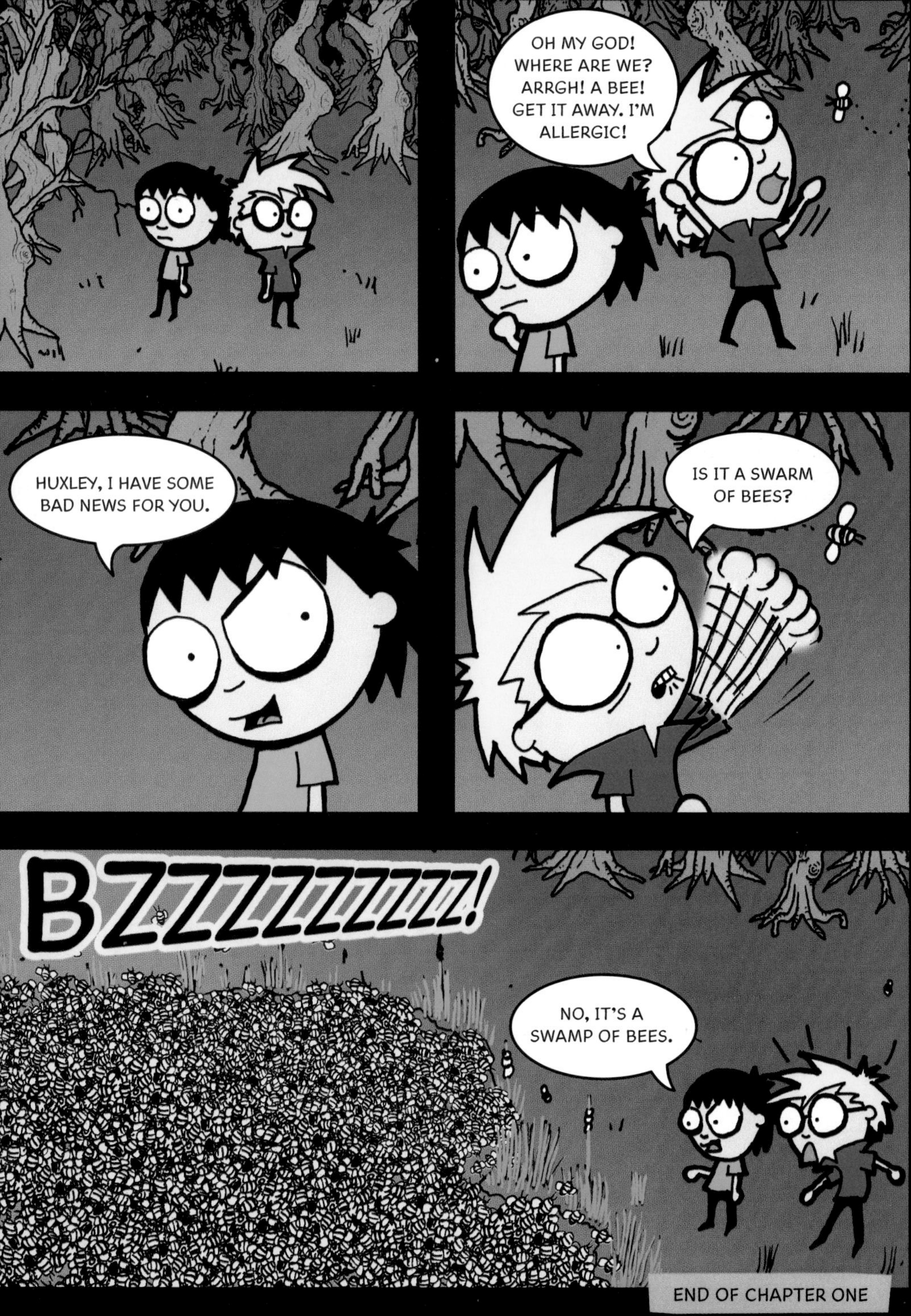
OH MY GOD! WHERE ARE WE? ARRGH! A BEE! GET IT AWAY. I'M ALLERGIC!
HUXLEY, I HAVE SOME BAD NEWS FOR YOU.
IS IT A SWARM OF BEES?
BZZZZZZZZZZ!
NO, IT'S A SWAMP OF BEES.
END OF CHAPTER ONE

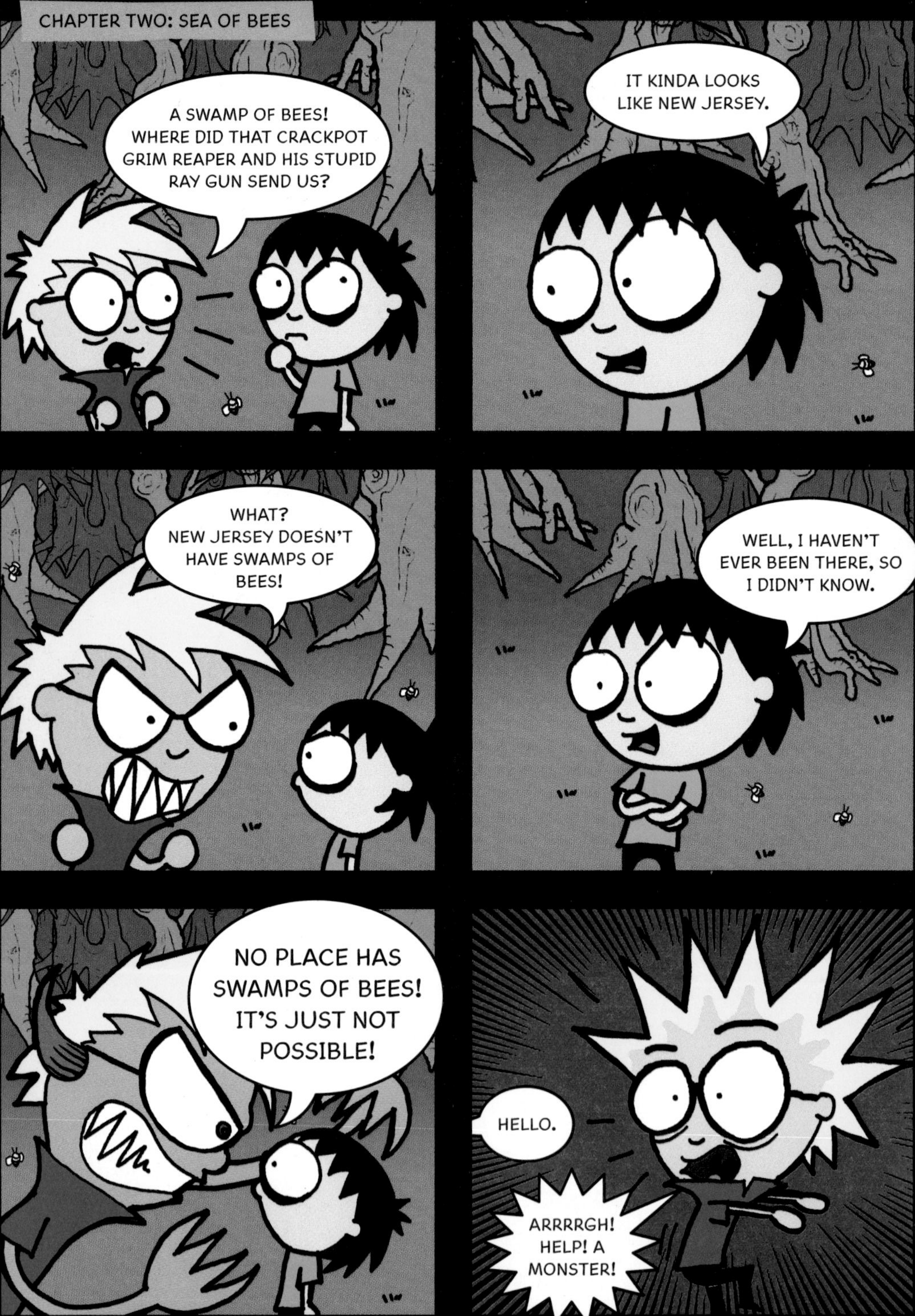
A SWAMP OF BEES! WHERE DID THAT CRACKPOT GRIM REAPER AND HIS STUPID RAY GUN SEND US?
IT KINDA LOOKS LIKE NEW JERSEY.
WHAT? NEW JERSEY DOESN'T HAVE SWAMPS OF BEES!
WELL, I HAVEN'T EVER BEEN THERE, SO I DIDN'T KNOW.
NO PLACE HAS SWAMPS OF BEES! IT'S JUST NOT POSSIBLE!
HELLO.
ARRRRGH! HELP! A MONSTER!

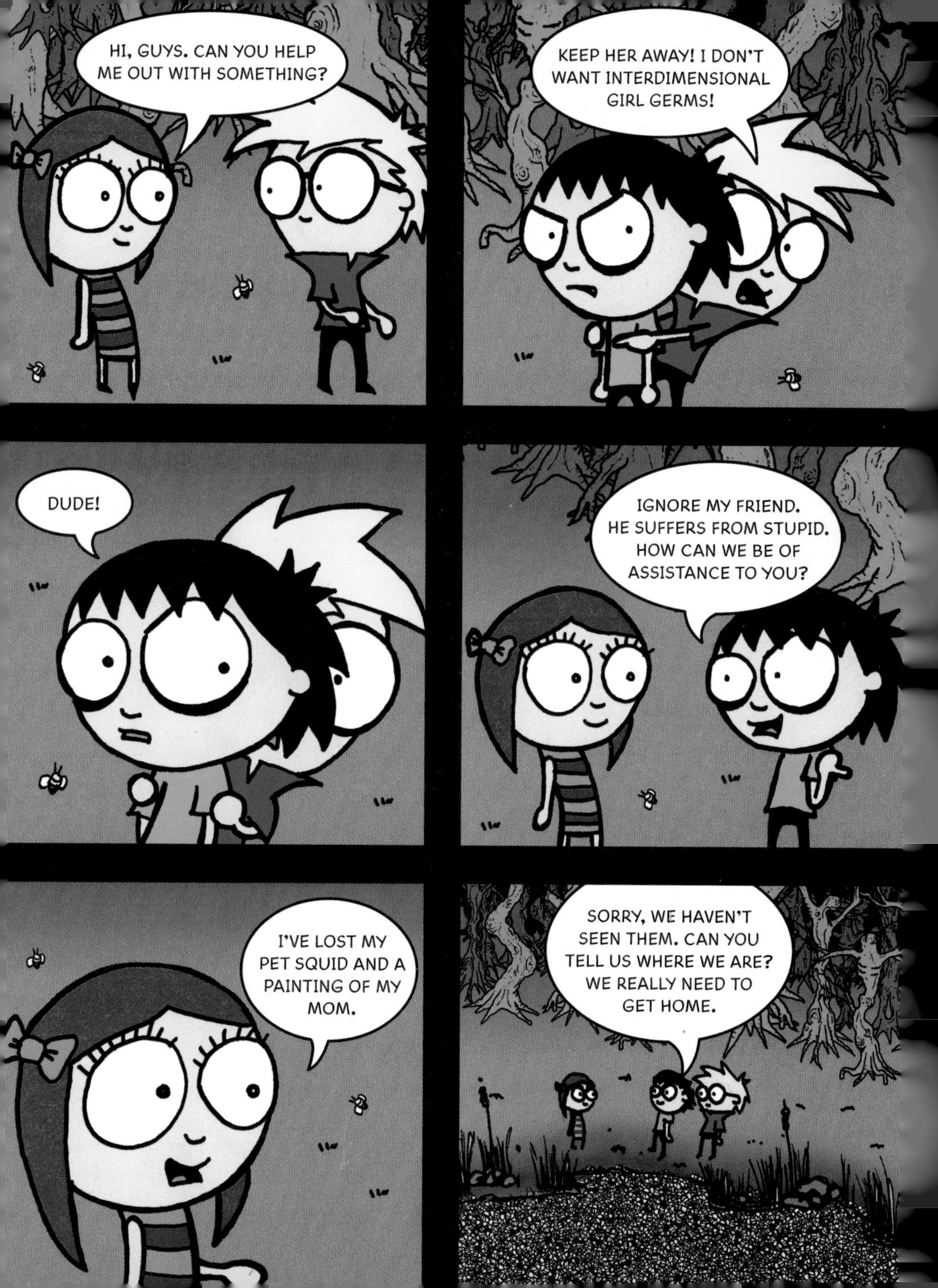
HI, GUYS. CAN YOU HELP ME OUT WITH SOMETHING?
KEEP HER AWAY! I DON'T WANT INTERDIMENSIONAL GIRL GERMS!
DUDE!
IGNORE MY FRIEND. HE SUFFERS FROM STUPID. HOW CAN WE BE OF ASSISTANCE TO YOU?
I'VE LOST MY PET SQUID AND A PAINTING OF MY MOM.
SORRY, WE HAVEN'T SEEN THEM. CAN YOU TELL US WHERE WE ARE? WE REALLY NEED TO GET HOME.

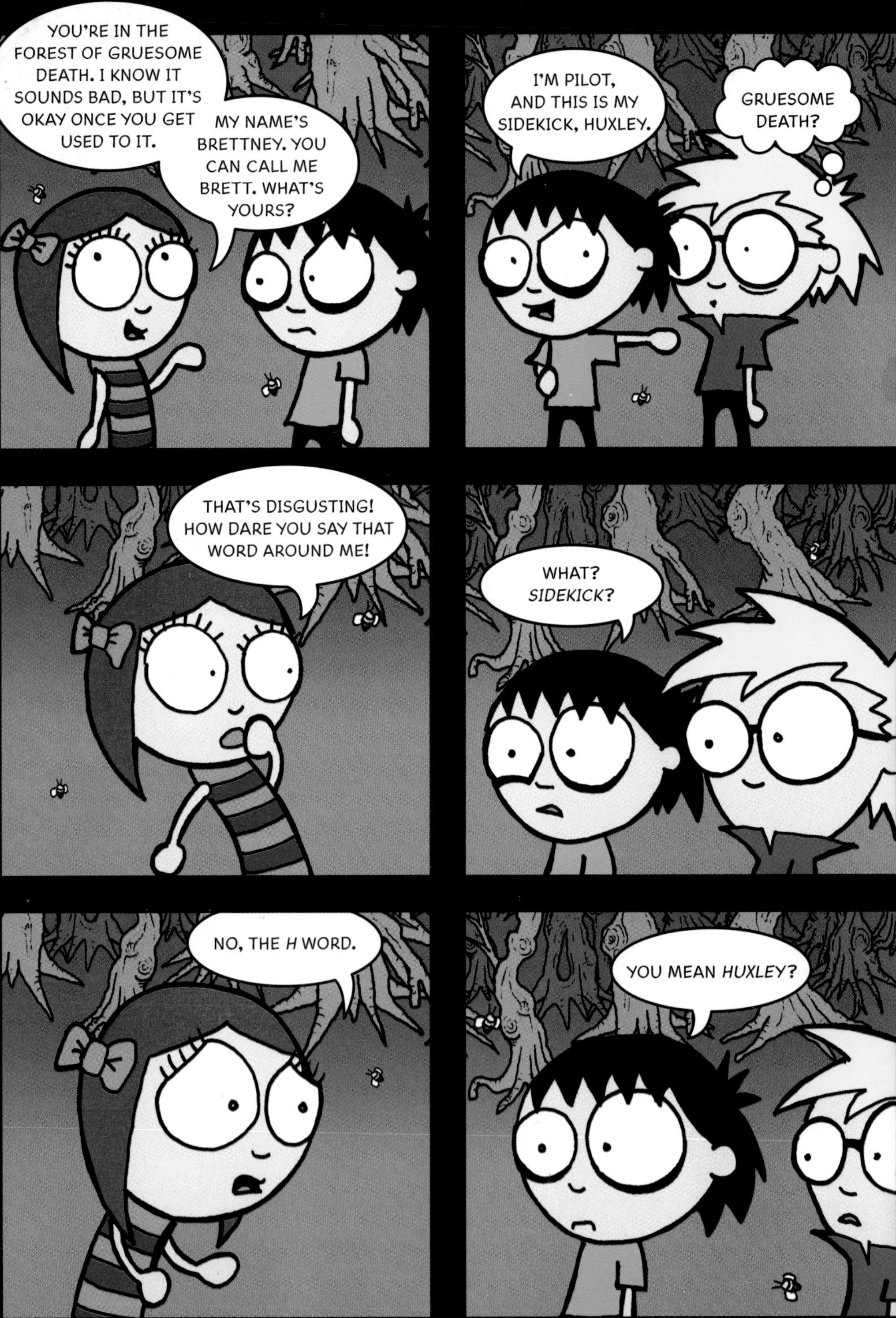
YOU'RE IN THE FOREST OF GRUESOME DEATH. I KNOW IT SOUNDS BAD, BUT IT'S OKAY ONCE YOU GET USED TO IT.
MY NAME'S BRETTNEY. YOU CAN CALL ME BRETT. WHAT'S YOURS?
I'M PILOT, AND THIS IS MY SIDEKICK, HUXLEY.
GRUESOME DEATH?
THAT'S DISGUSTING! HOW DARE YOU SAY THAT WORD AROUND ME!
WHAT? *SIDEKICK*?
NO, THE *H* WORD.
YOU MEAN *HUXLEY*?

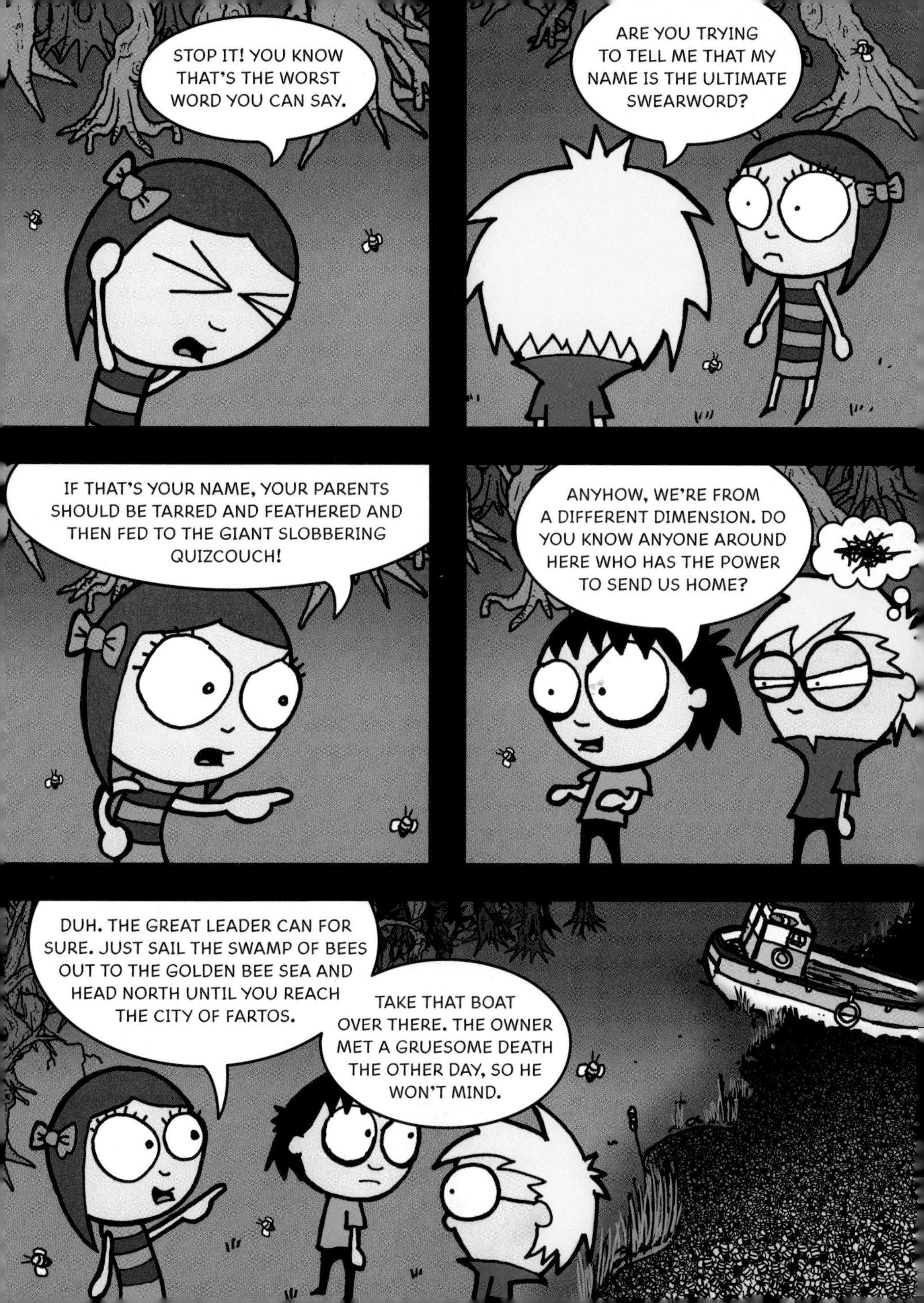
STOP IT! YOU KNOW THAT'S THE WORST WORD YOU CAN SAY.
ARE YOU TRYING TO TELL ME THAT MY NAME IS THE ULTIMATE SWEARWORD?
IF THAT'S YOUR NAME, YOUR PARENTS SHOULD BE TARRED AND FEATHERED AND THEN FED TO THE GIANT SLOBBERING QUIZCOUCH!
ANYHOW, WE'RE FROM A DIFFERENT DIMENSION. DO YOU KNOW ANYONE AROUND HERE WHO HAS THE POWER TO SEND US HOME?
DUH. THE GREAT LEADER CAN FOR SURE. JUST SAIL THE SWAMP OF BEES OUT TO THE GOLDEN BEE SEA AND HEAD NORTH UNTIL YOU REACH THE CITY OF FARTOS.
TAKE THAT BOAT OVER THERE. THE OWNER MET A GRUESOME DEATH THE OTHER DAY, SO HE WON'T MIND.

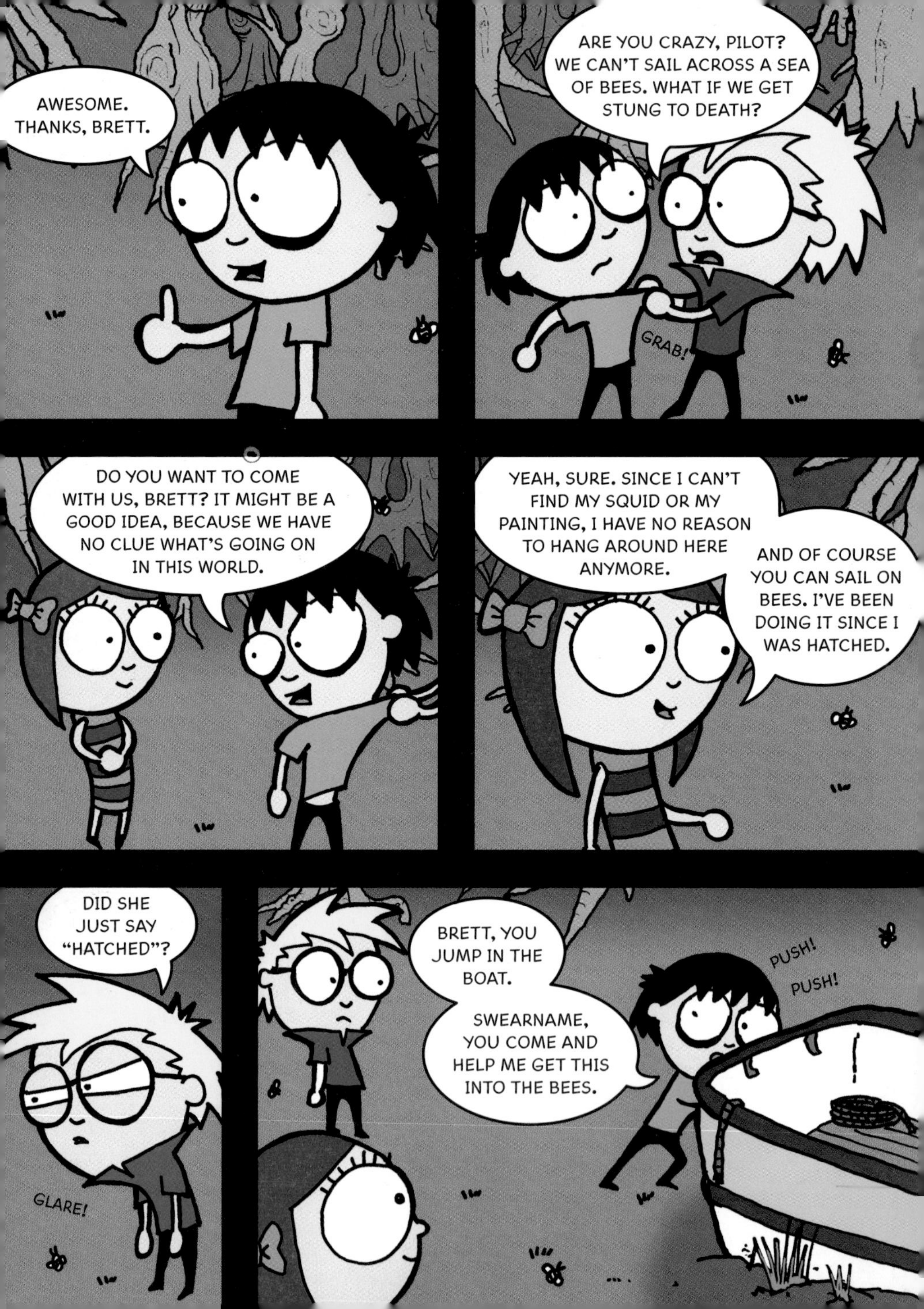

AWESOME. THANKS, BRETT.
ARE YOU CRAZY, PILOT? WE CAN'T SAIL ACROSS A SEA OF BEES. WHAT IF WE GET STUNG TO DEATH?
GRAB!
DO YOU WANT TO COME WITH US, BRETT? IT MIGHT BE A GOOD IDEA, BECAUSE WE HAVE NO CLUE WHAT'S GOING ON IN THIS WORLD.
YEAH, SURE. SINCE I CAN'T FIND MY SQUID OR MY PAINTING, I HAVE NO REASON TO HANG AROUND HERE ANYMORE.
AND OF COURSE YOU CAN SAIL ON BEES. I'VE BEEN DOING IT SINCE I WAS HATCHED.
DID SHE JUST SAY "HATCHED"?
GLARE!
BRETT, YOU JUMP IN THE BOAT.
SWEARNAME, YOU COME AND HELP ME GET THIS INTO THE BEES.
PUSH!
PUSH!

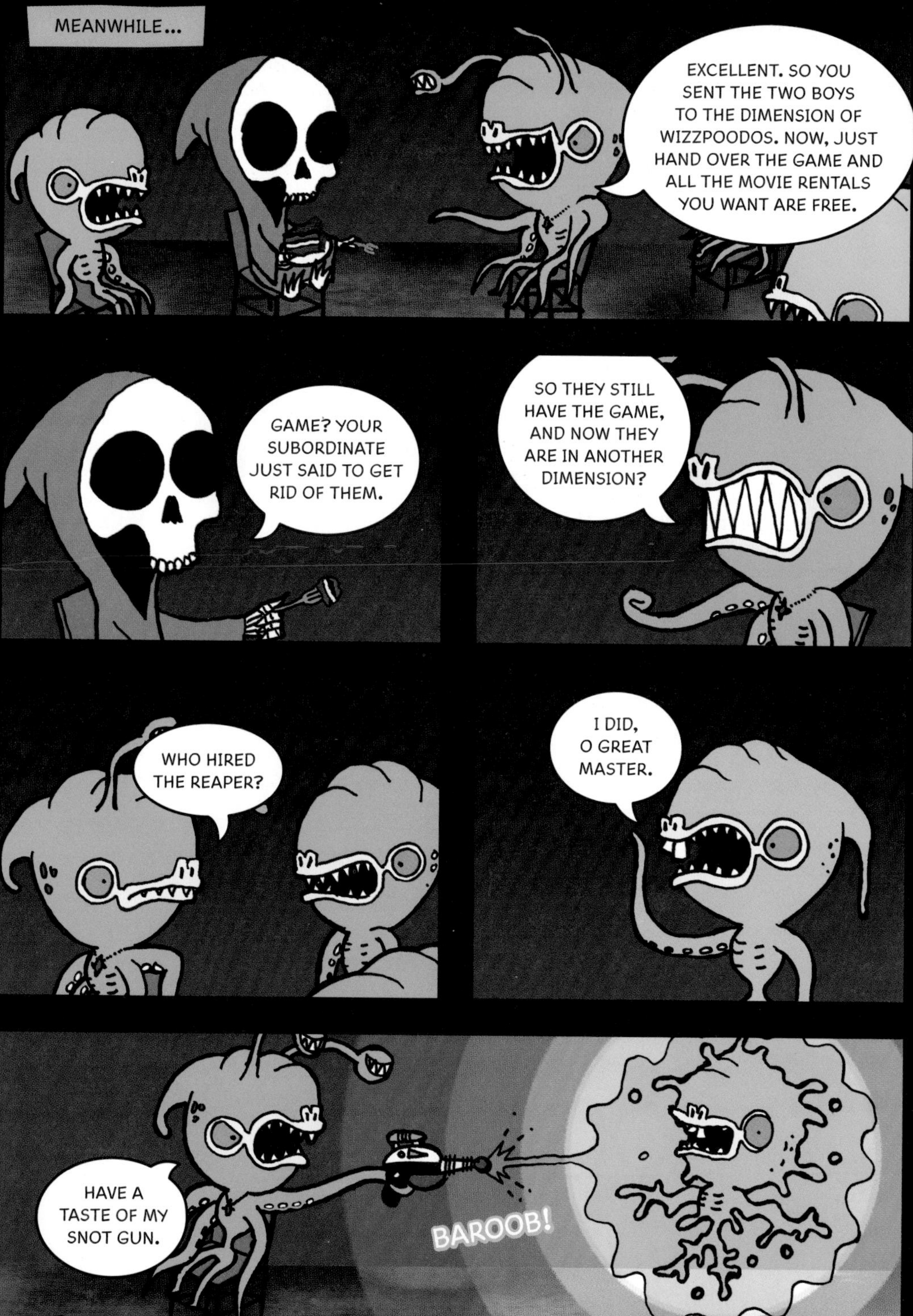

MEANWHILE...
EXCELLENT. SO YOU SENT THE TWO BOYS TO THE DIMENSION OF WIZZPOODOS. NOW, JUST HAND OVER THE GAME AND ALL THE MOVIE RENTALS YOU WANT ARE FREE.
GAME? YOUR SUBORDINATE JUST SAID TO GET RID OF THEM.
SO THEY STILL HAVE THE GAME, AND NOW THEY ARE IN ANOTHER DIMENSION?
WHO HIRED THE REAPER?
I DID, O GREAT MASTER.
HAVE A TASTE OF MY SNOT GUN.
BAROOB!

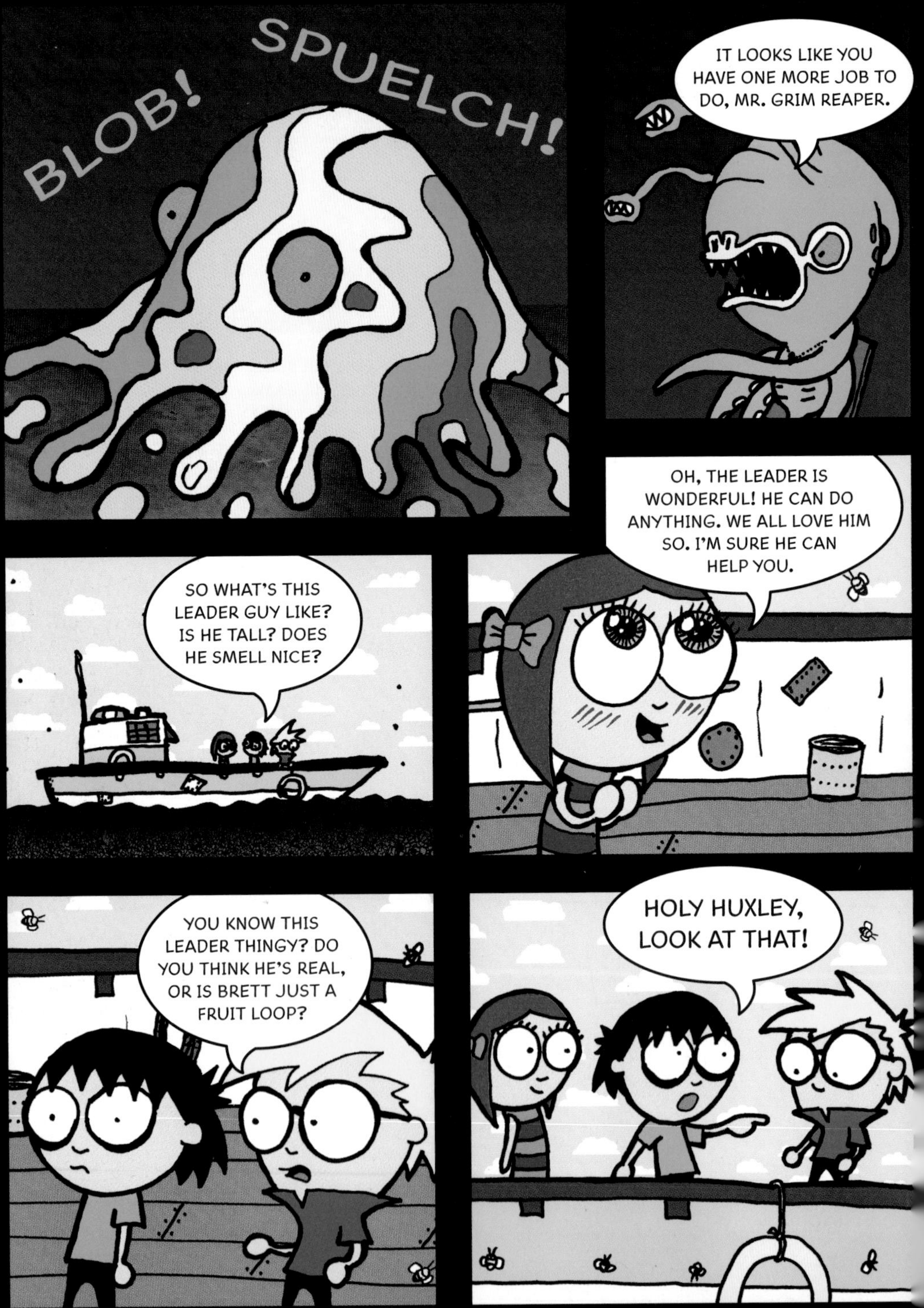
BLOB!
SPUELCH!
IT LOOKS LIKE YOU HAVE ONE MORE JOB TO DO, MR. GRIM REAPER.
SO WHAT'S THIS LEADER GUY LIKE? IS HE TALL? DOES HE SMELL NICE?
OH, THE LEADER IS WONDERFUL! HE CAN DO ANYTHING. WE ALL LOVE HIM SO. I'M SURE HE CAN HELP YOU.
YOU KNOW THIS LEADER THINGY? DO YOU THINK HE'S REAL, OR IS BRETT JUST A FRUIT LOOP?
HOLY HUXLEY, LOOK AT THAT!

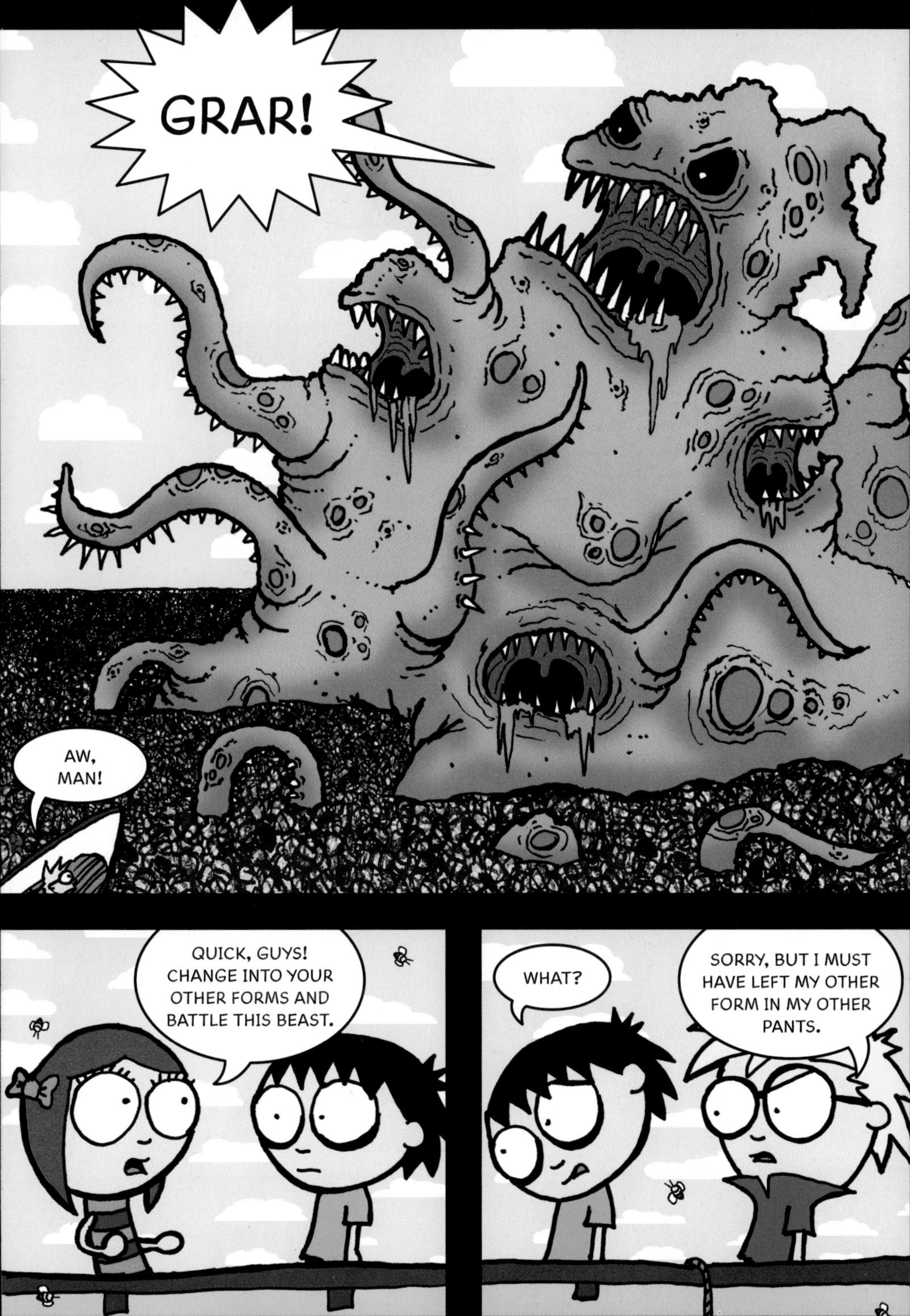
GRAR!
AW, MAN!
QUICK, GUYS! CHANGE INTO YOUR OTHER FORMS AND BATTLE THIS BEAST.
WHAT?
SORRY, BUT I MUST HAVE LEFT MY OTHER FORM IN MY OTHER PANTS.

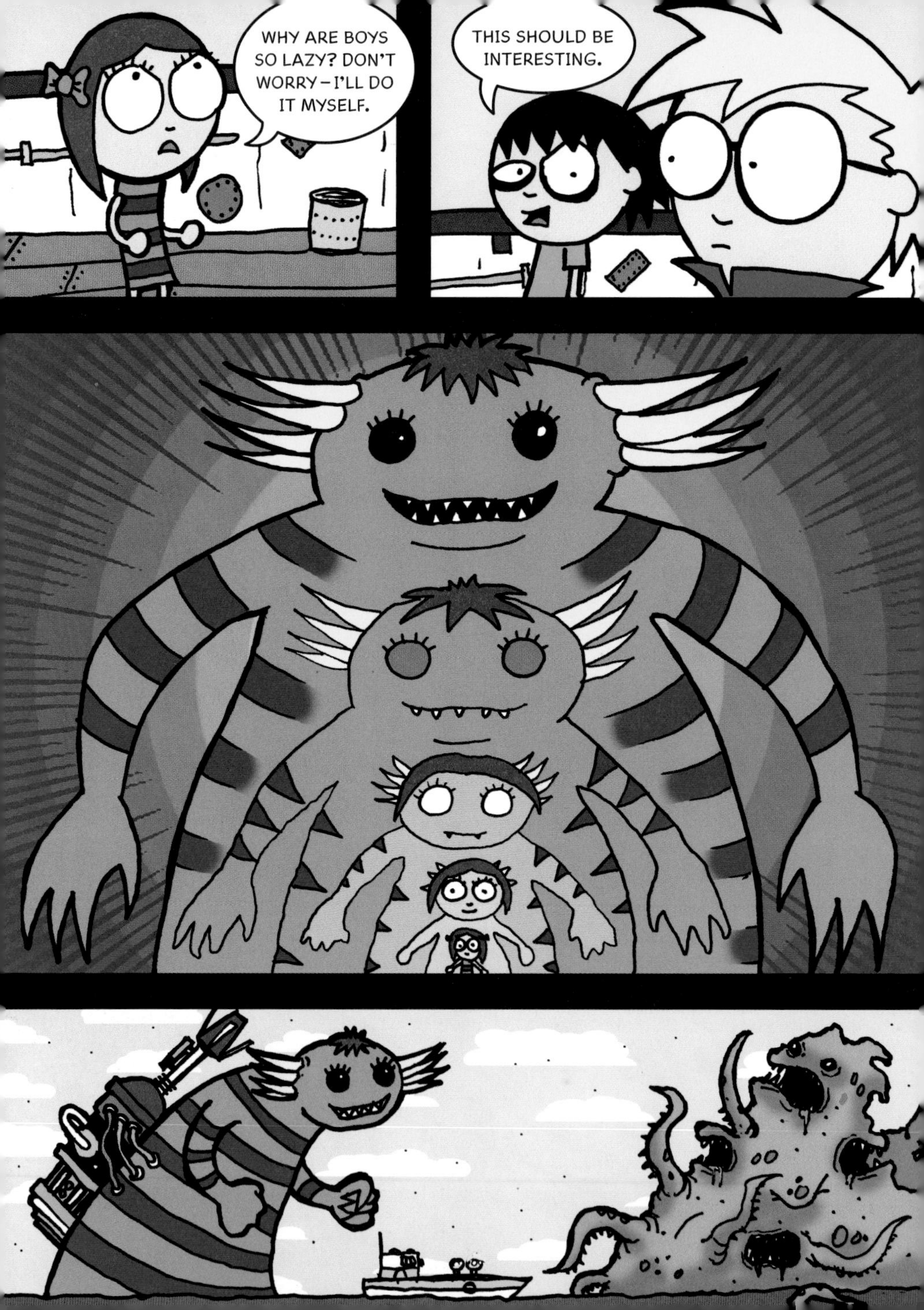
WHY ARE BOYS SO LAZY? DON'T WORRY–I'LL DO IT MYSELF.
THIS SHOULD BE INTERESTING.

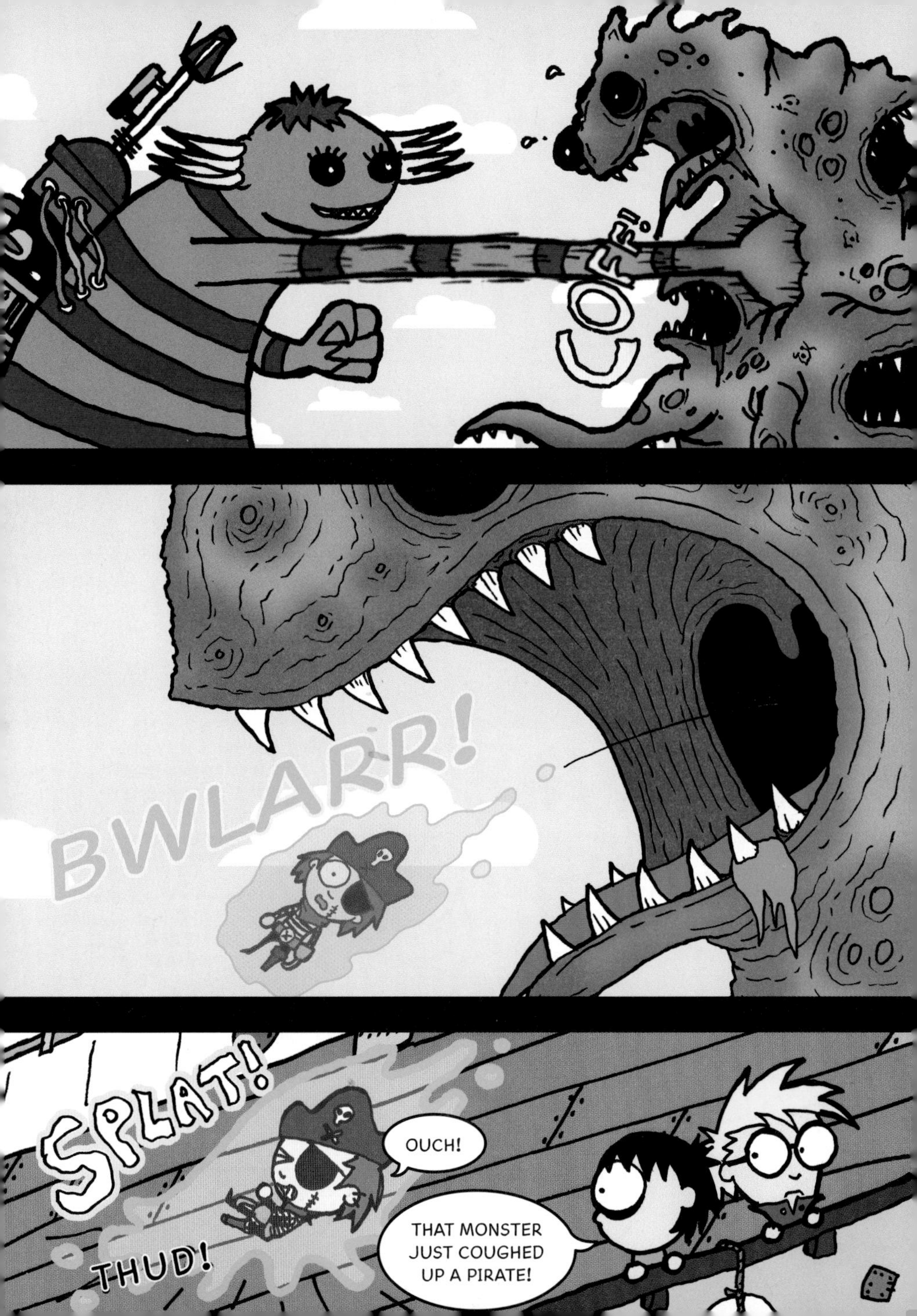
COFF!
BWLARR!
SPLAT!
THUD!
OUCH!
THAT MONSTER JUST COUGHED UP A PIRATE!

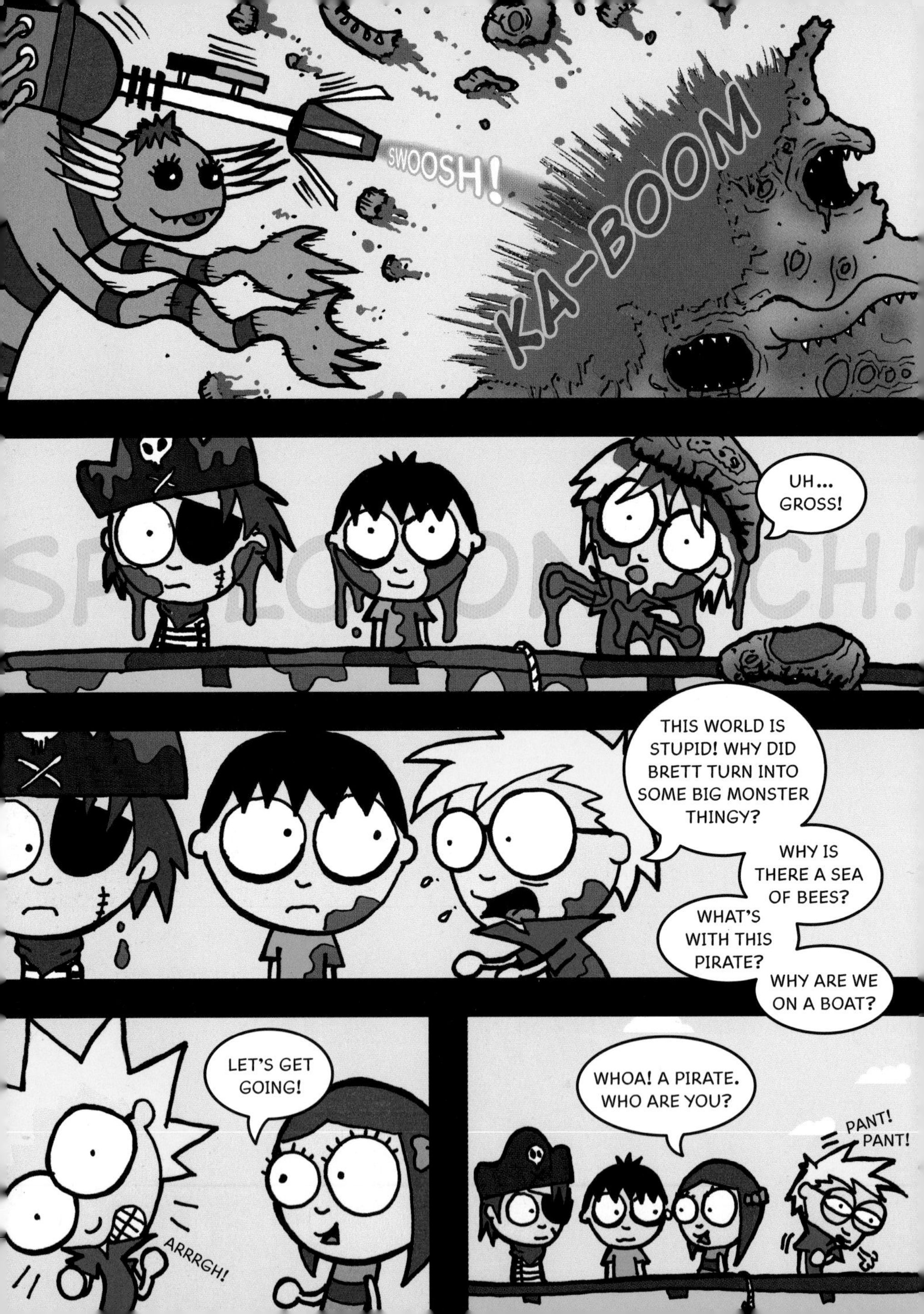

SWOOSH!
KA-BOOM
UH... GROSS!
THIS WORLD IS STUPID! WHY DID BRETT TURN INTO SOME BIG MONSTER THINGY?
WHY IS THERE A SEA OF BEES?
WHAT'S WITH THIS PIRATE?
WHY ARE WE ON A BOAT?
LET'S GET GOING!
ARRRGH!
WHOA! A PIRATE. WHO ARE YOU?
PANT! PANT!

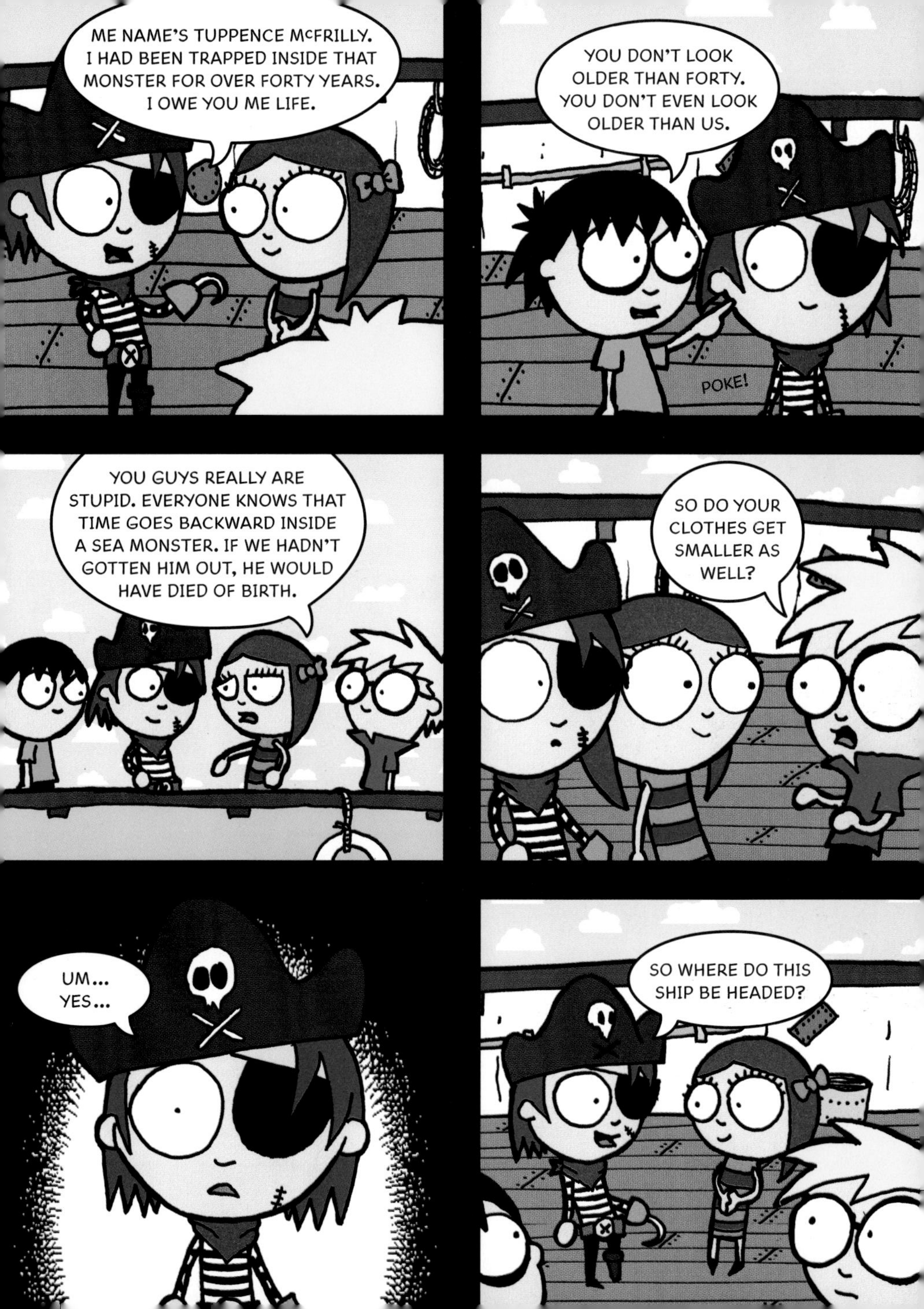
ME NAME'S TUPPENCE McFRILLY. I HAD BEEN TRAPPED INSIDE THAT MONSTER FOR OVER FORTY YEARS. I OWE YOU ME LIFE.
YOU DON'T LOOK OLDER THAN FORTY. YOU DON'T EVEN LOOK OLDER THAN US.
POKE!
YOU GUYS REALLY ARE STUPID. EVERYONE KNOWS THAT TIME GOES BACKWARD INSIDE A SEA MONSTER. IF WE HADN'T GOTTEN HIM OUT, HE WOULD HAVE DIED OF BIRTH.
SO DO YOUR CLOTHES GET SMALLER AS WELL?
UM... YES...
SO WHERE DO THIS SHIP BE HEADED?

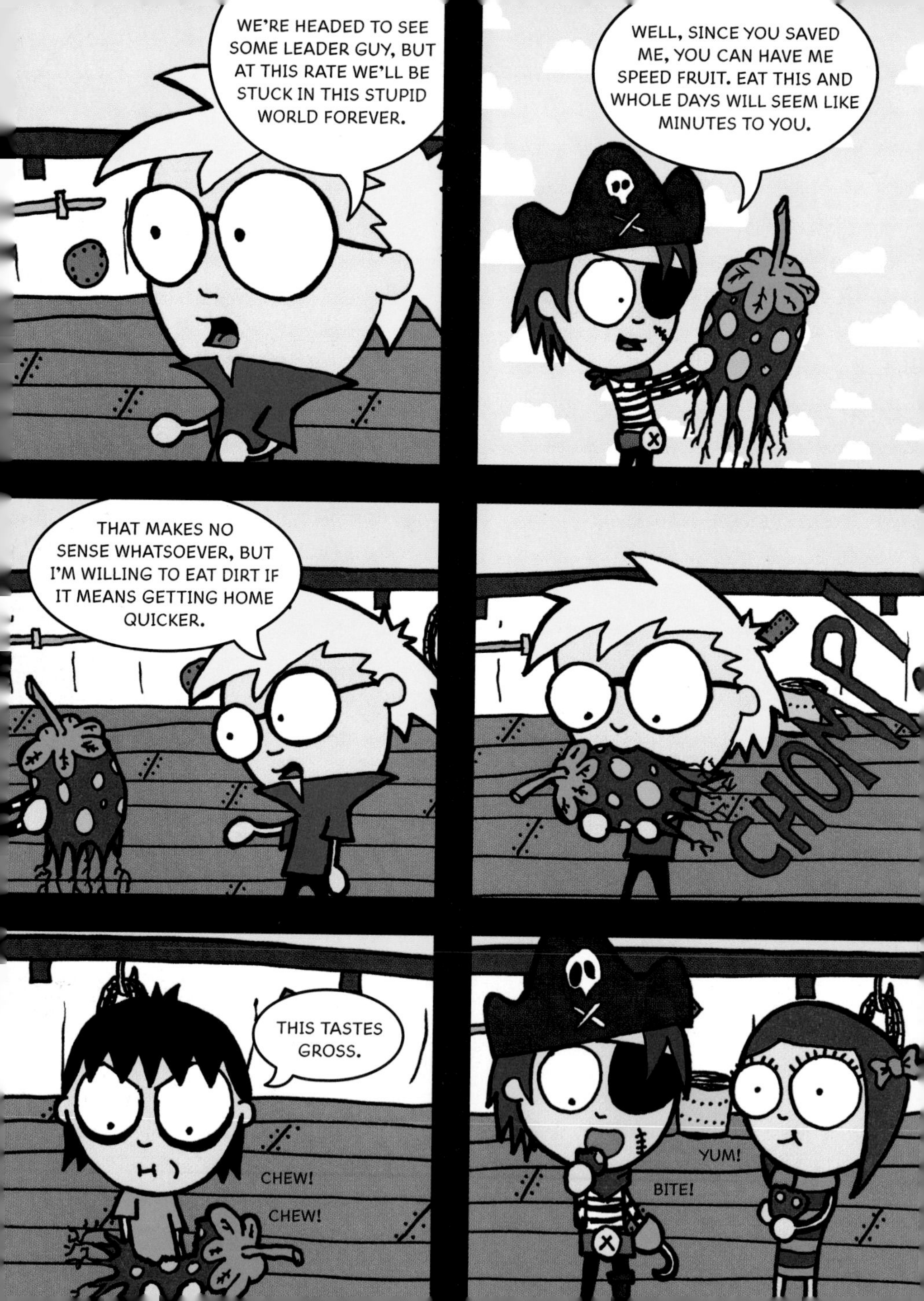
WE'RE HEADED TO SEE SOME LEADER GUY, BUT AT THIS RATE WE'LL BE STUCK IN THIS STUPID WORLD FOREVER.
WELL, SINCE YOU SAVED ME, YOU CAN HAVE ME SPEED FRUIT. EAT THIS AND WHOLE DAYS WILL SEEM LIKE MINUTES TO YOU.
THAT MAKES NO SENSE WHATSOEVER, BUT I'M WILLING TO EAT DIRT IF IT MEANS GETTING HOME QUICKER.
CHOMP!
THIS TASTES GROSS.
CHEW!
CHEW!
YUM!
BITE!

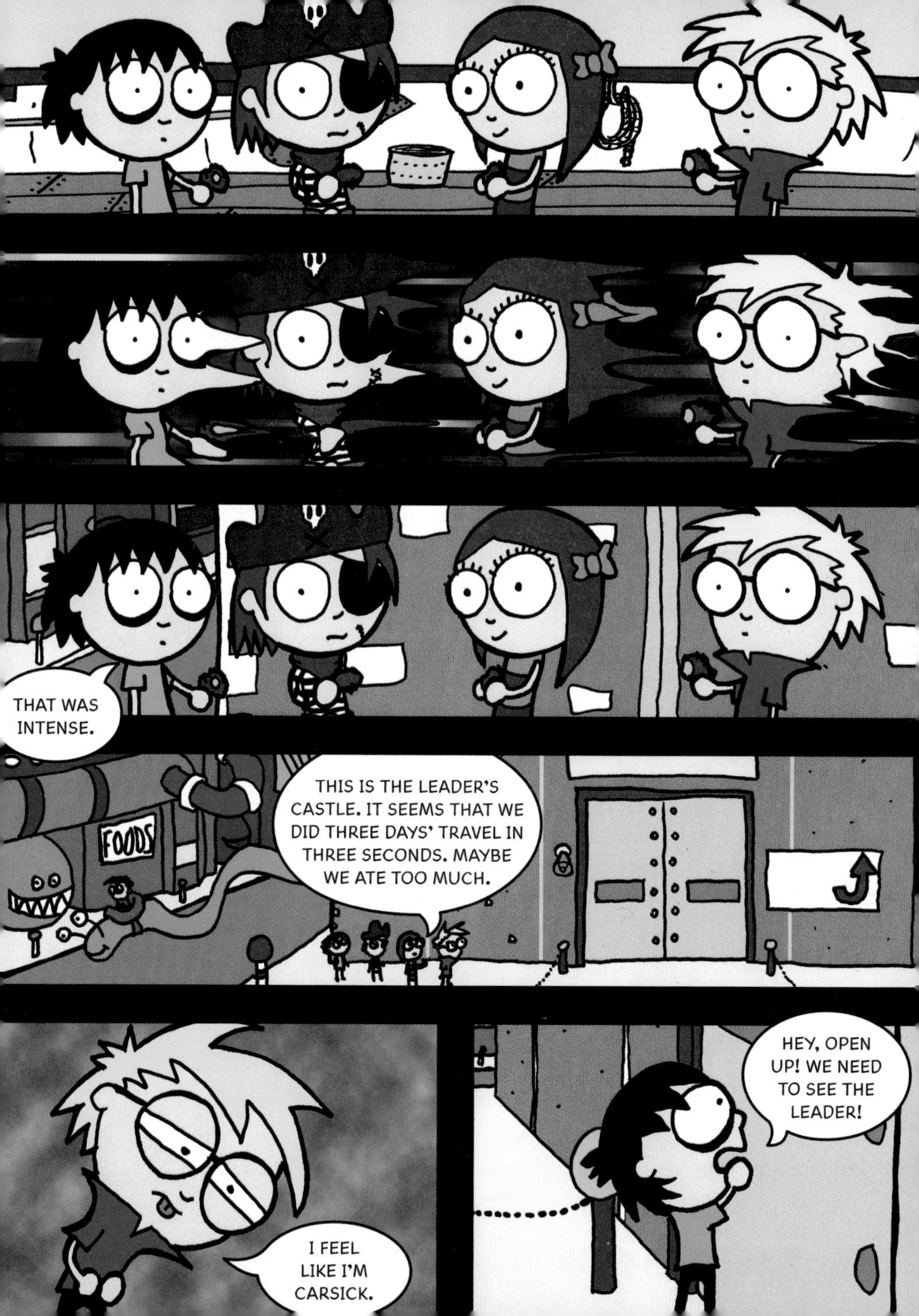
THAT WAS INTENSE.
THIS IS THE LEADER'S CASTLE. IT SEEMS THAT WE DID THREE DAYS' TRAVEL IN THREE SECONDS. MAYBE WE ATE TOO MUCH.
FOODS
I FEEL LIKE I'M CARSICK.
HEY, OPEN UP! WE NEED TO SEE THE LEADER!

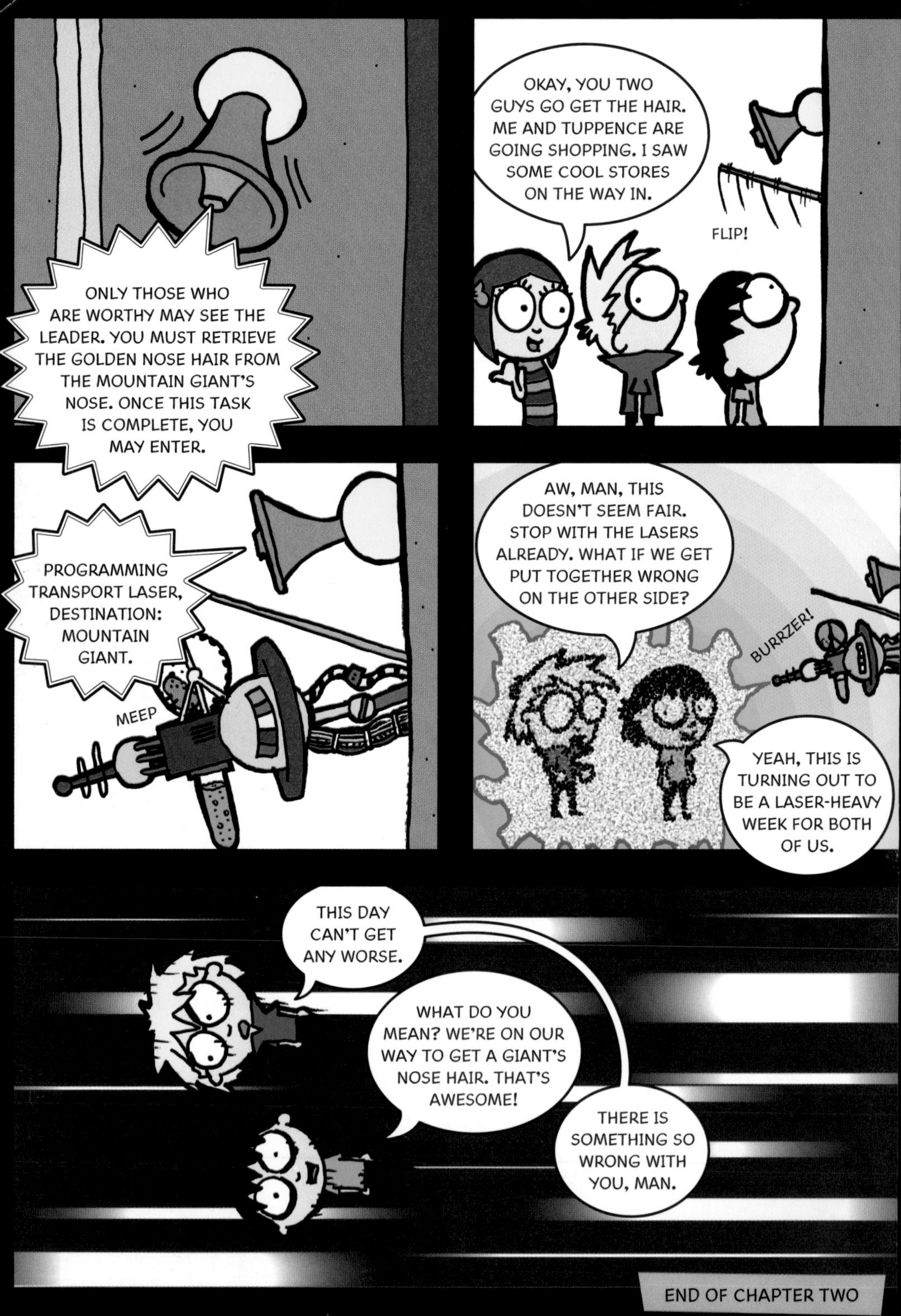
ONLY THOSE WHO ARE WORTHY MAY SEE THE LEADER. YOU MUST RETRIEVE THE GOLDEN NOSE HAIR FROM THE MOUNTAIN GIANT'S NOSE. ONCE THIS TASK IS COMPLETE, YOU MAY ENTER.
OKAY, YOU TWO GUYS GO GET THE HAIR. ME AND TUPPENCE ARE GOING SHOPPING. I SAW SOME COOL STORES ON THE WAY IN.
FLIP!
PROGRAMMING TRANSPORT LASER, DESTINATION: MOUNTAIN GIANT.
MEEP
AW, MAN, THIS DOESN'T SEEM FAIR. STOP WITH THE LASERS ALREADY. WHAT IF WE GET PUT TOGETHER WRONG ON THE OTHER SIDE?
BURRZER!
YEAH, THIS IS TURNING OUT TO BE A LASER-HEAVY WEEK FOR BOTH OF US.
THIS DAY CAN'T GET ANY WORSE.
WHAT DO YOU MEAN? WE'RE ON OUR WAY TO GET A GIANT'S NOSE HAIR. THAT'S AWESOME!
THERE IS SOMETHING SO WRONG WITH YOU, MAN.
END OF CHAPTER TWO

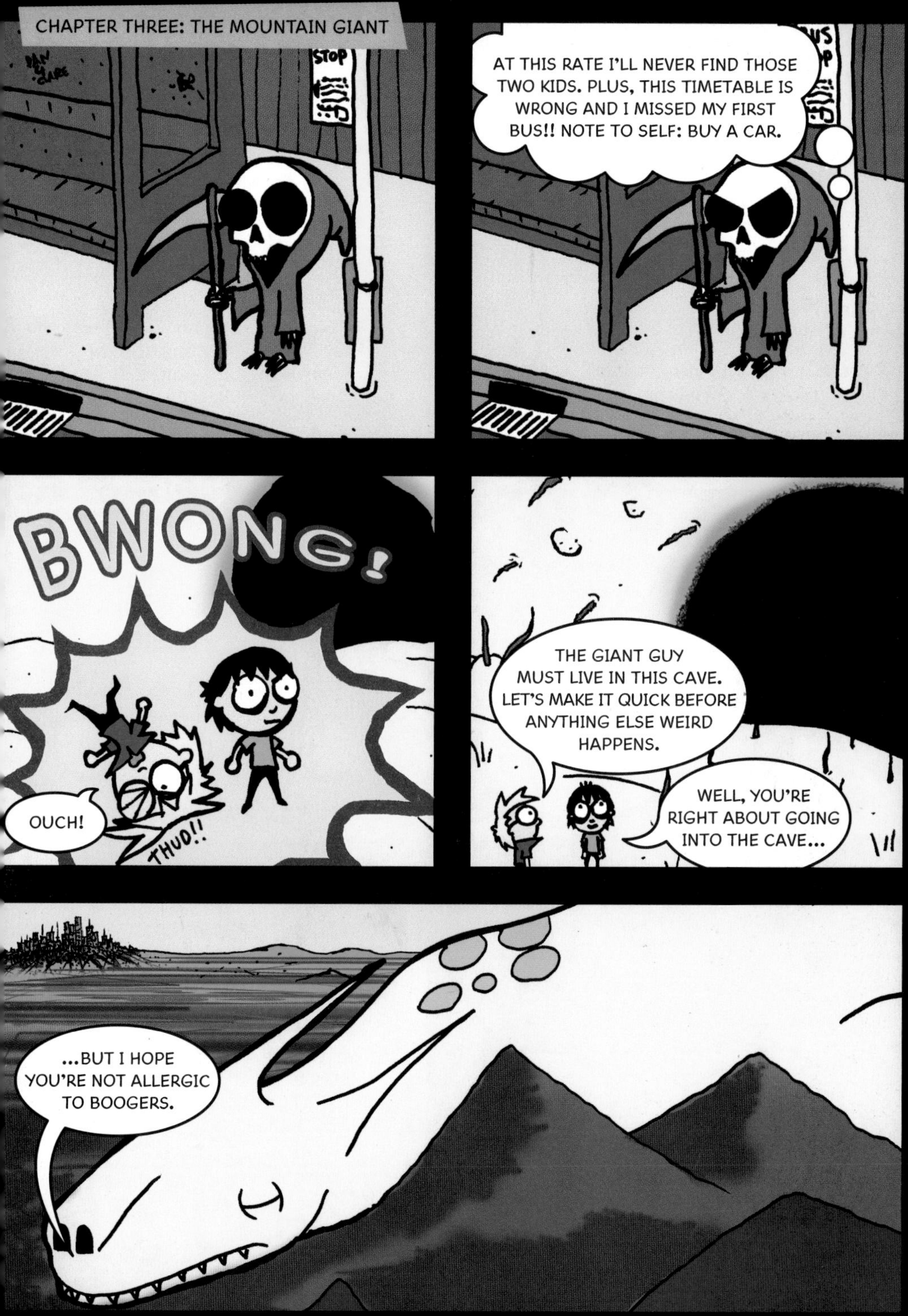
CHAPTER THREE: THE MOUNTAIN GIANT
STOP
AT THIS RATE I'LL NEVER FIND THOSE TWO KIDS. PLUS, THIS TIMETABLE IS WRONG AND I MISSED MY FIRST BUS!! NOTE TO SELF: BUY A CAR.
BWONG!
OUCH!
THUD!!
THE GIANT GUY MUST LIVE IN THIS CAVE. LET'S MAKE IT QUICK BEFORE ANYTHING ELSE WEIRD HAPPENS.
WELL, YOU'RE RIGHT ABOUT GOING INTO THE CAVE...
...BUT I HOPE YOU'RE NOT ALLERGIC TO BOOGERS.

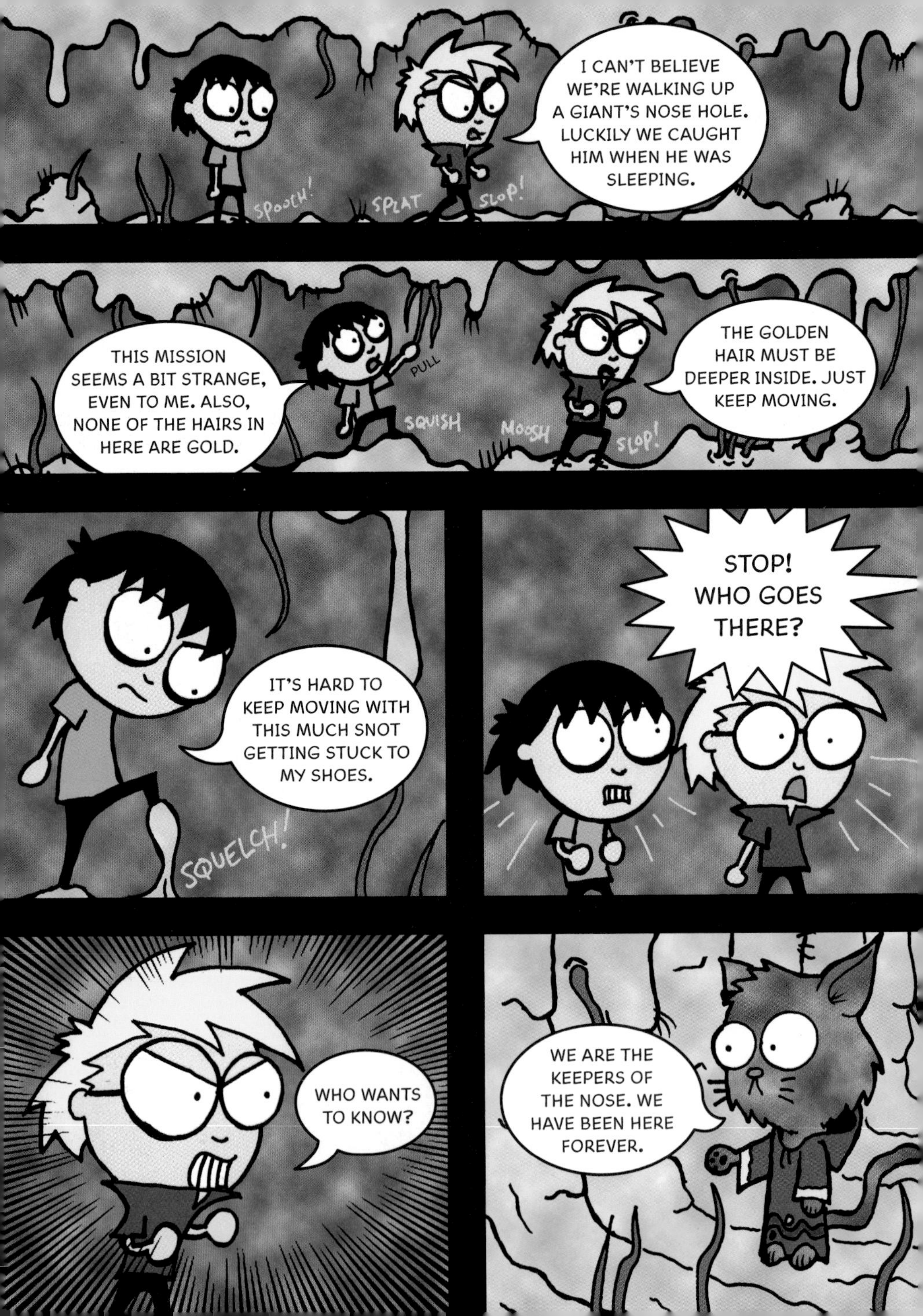
I CAN'T BELIEVE WE'RE WALKING UP A GIANT'S NOSE HOLE. LUCKILY WE CAUGHT HIM WHEN HE WAS SLEEPING.
SPOOCH!
SPLAT
SLOP!
THIS MISSION SEEMS A BIT STRANGE, EVEN TO ME. ALSO, NONE OF THE HAIRS IN HERE ARE GOLD.
PULL
SQUISH
MOOSH
SLOP!
THE GOLDEN HAIR MUST BE DEEPER INSIDE. JUST KEEP MOVING.
IT'S HARD TO KEEP MOVING WITH THIS MUCH SNOT GETTING STUCK TO MY SHOES.
SQUELCH!
STOP! WHO GOES THERE?
WHO WANTS TO KNOW?
WE ARE THE KEEPERS OF THE NOSE. WE HAVE BEEN HERE FOREVER.

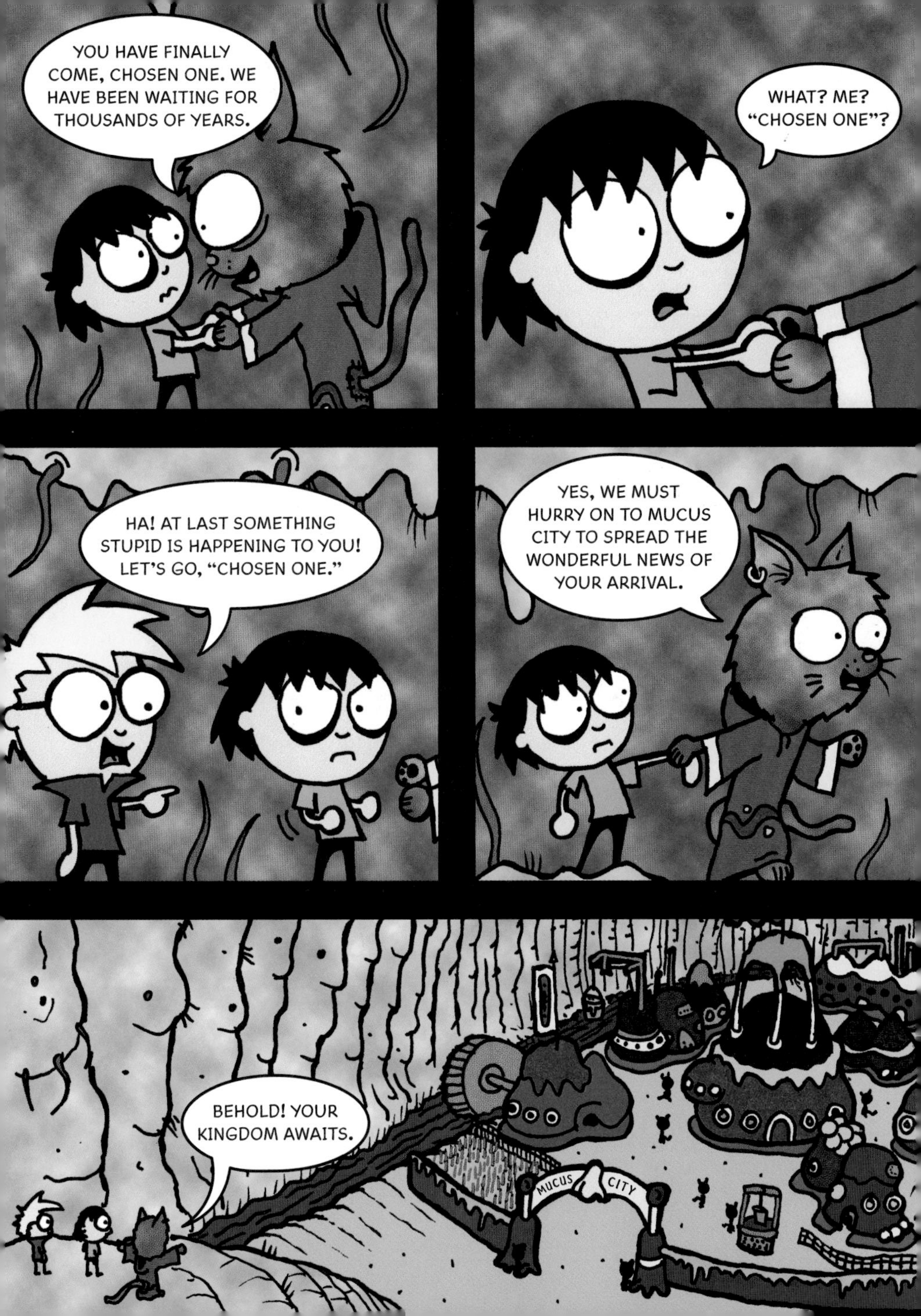
YOU HAVE FINALLY COME, CHOSEN ONE. WE HAVE BEEN WAITING FOR THOUSANDS OF YEARS.
WHAT? ME? "CHOSEN ONE"?
HA! AT LAST SOMETHING STUPID IS HAPPENING TO YOU! LET'S GO, "CHOSEN ONE."
YES, WE MUST HURRY ON TO MUCUS CITY TO SPREAD THE WONDERFUL NEWS OF YOUR ARRIVAL.
BEHOLD! YOUR KINGDOM AWAITS.
MUCUS CITY

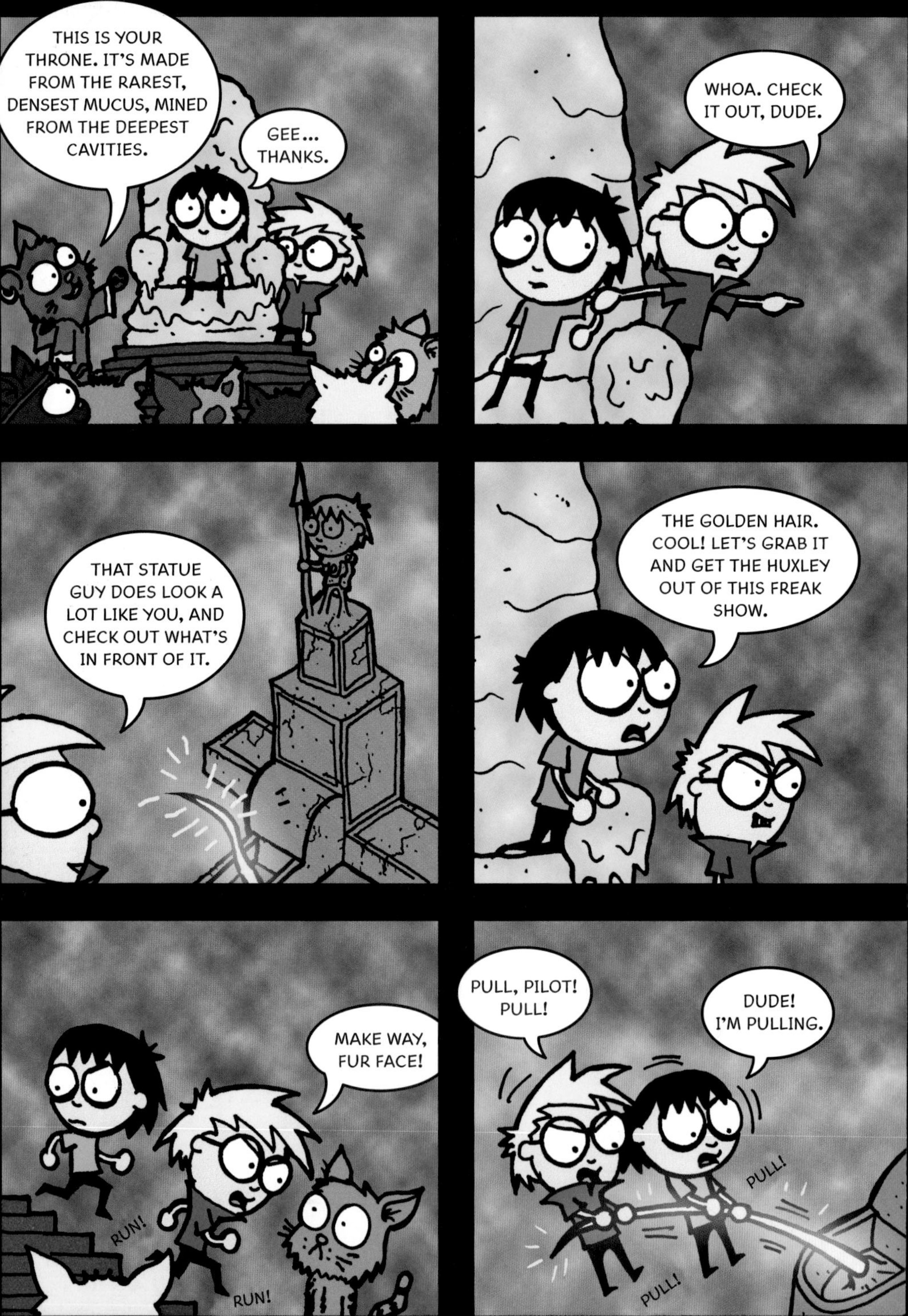
THIS IS YOUR THRONE. IT'S MADE FROM THE RAREST, DENSEST MUCUS, MINED FROM THE DEEPEST CAVITIES.
GEE... THANKS.
WHOA. CHECK IT OUT, DUDE.
THAT STATUE GUY DOES LOOK A LOT LIKE YOU, AND CHECK OUT WHAT'S IN FRONT OF IT.
THE GOLDEN HAIR. COOL! LET'S GRAB IT AND GET THE HUXLEY OUT OF THIS FREAK SHOW.
MAKE WAY, FUR FACE!
RUN!
RUN!
PULL, PILOT! PULL!
DUDE! I'M PULLING.
PULL!
PULL!

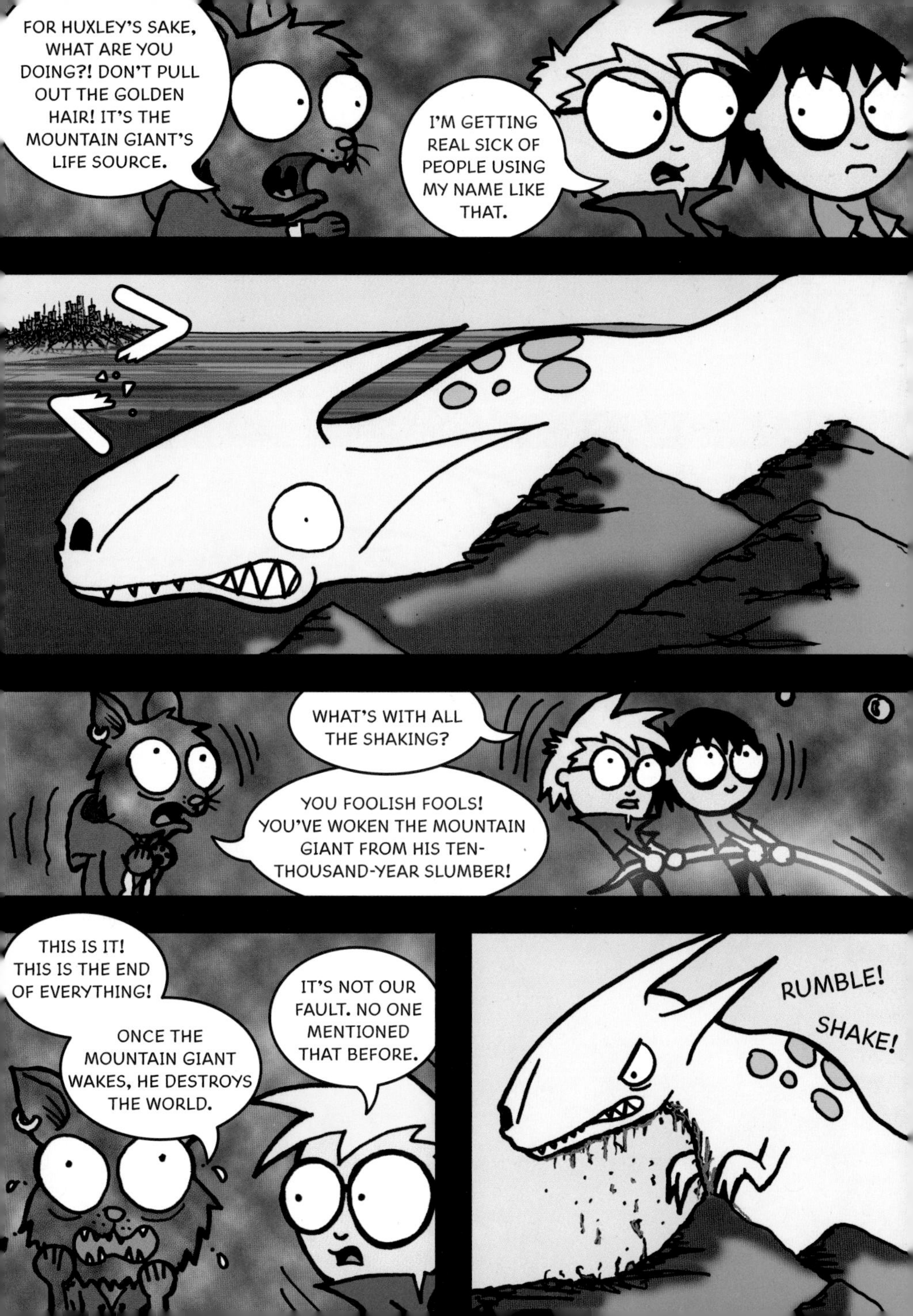
FOR HUXLEY'S SAKE, WHAT ARE YOU DOING?! DON'T PULL OUT THE GOLDEN HAIR! IT'S THE MOUNTAIN GIANT'S LIFE SOURCE.
I'M GETTING REAL SICK OF PEOPLE USING MY NAME LIKE THAT.
WHAT'S WITH ALL THE SHAKING?
YOU FOOLISH FOOLS! YOU'VE WOKEN THE MOUNTAIN GIANT FROM HIS TEN-THOUSAND-YEAR SLUMBER!
THIS IS IT! THIS IS THE END OF EVERYTHING!
ONCE THE MOUNTAIN GIANT WAKES, HE DESTROYS THE WORLD.
IT'S NOT OUR FAULT. NO ONE MENTIONED THAT BEFORE.
RUMBLE!
SHAKE!

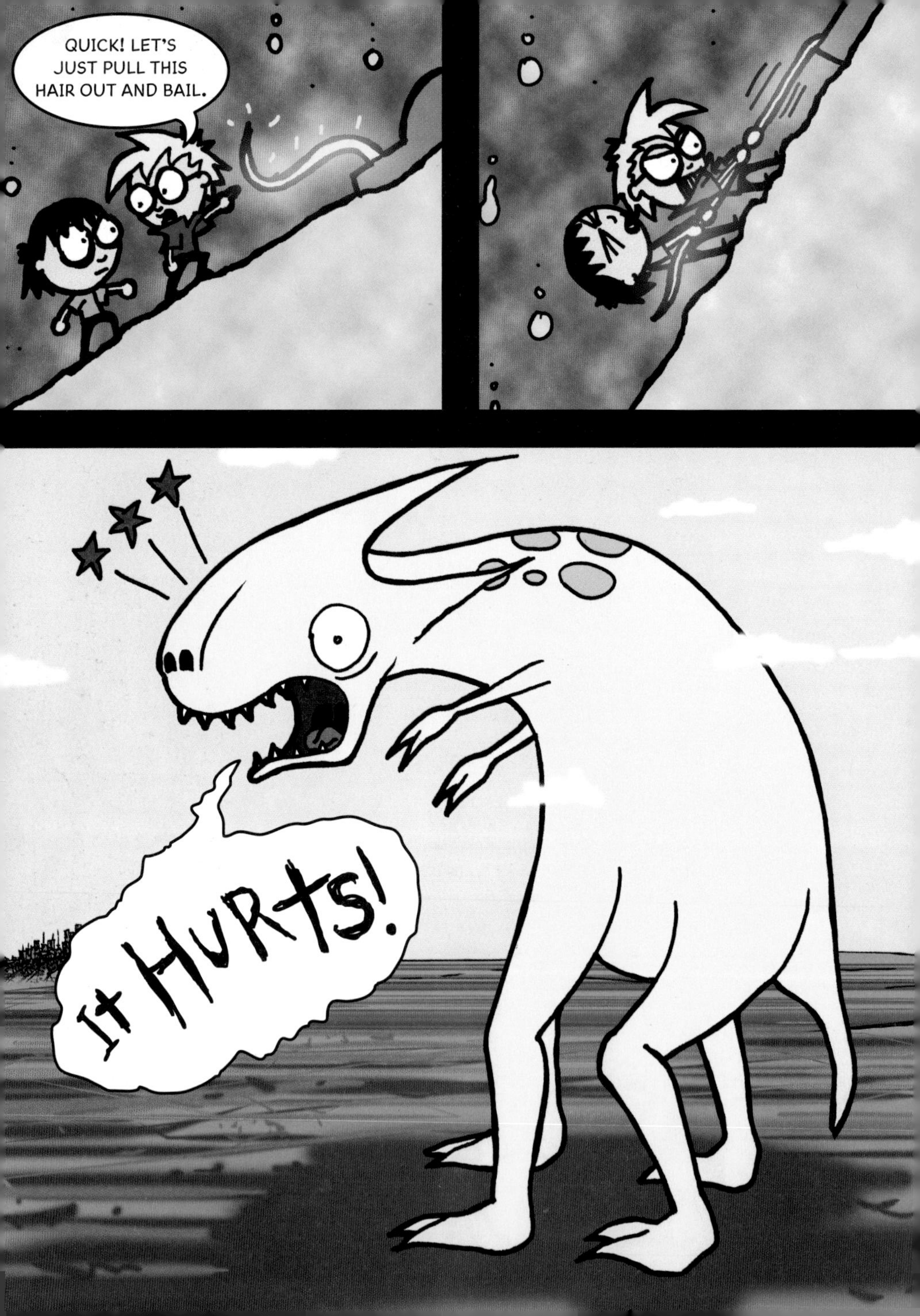
QUICK! LET'S JUST PULL THIS HAIR OUT AND BAIL.
It HURts!

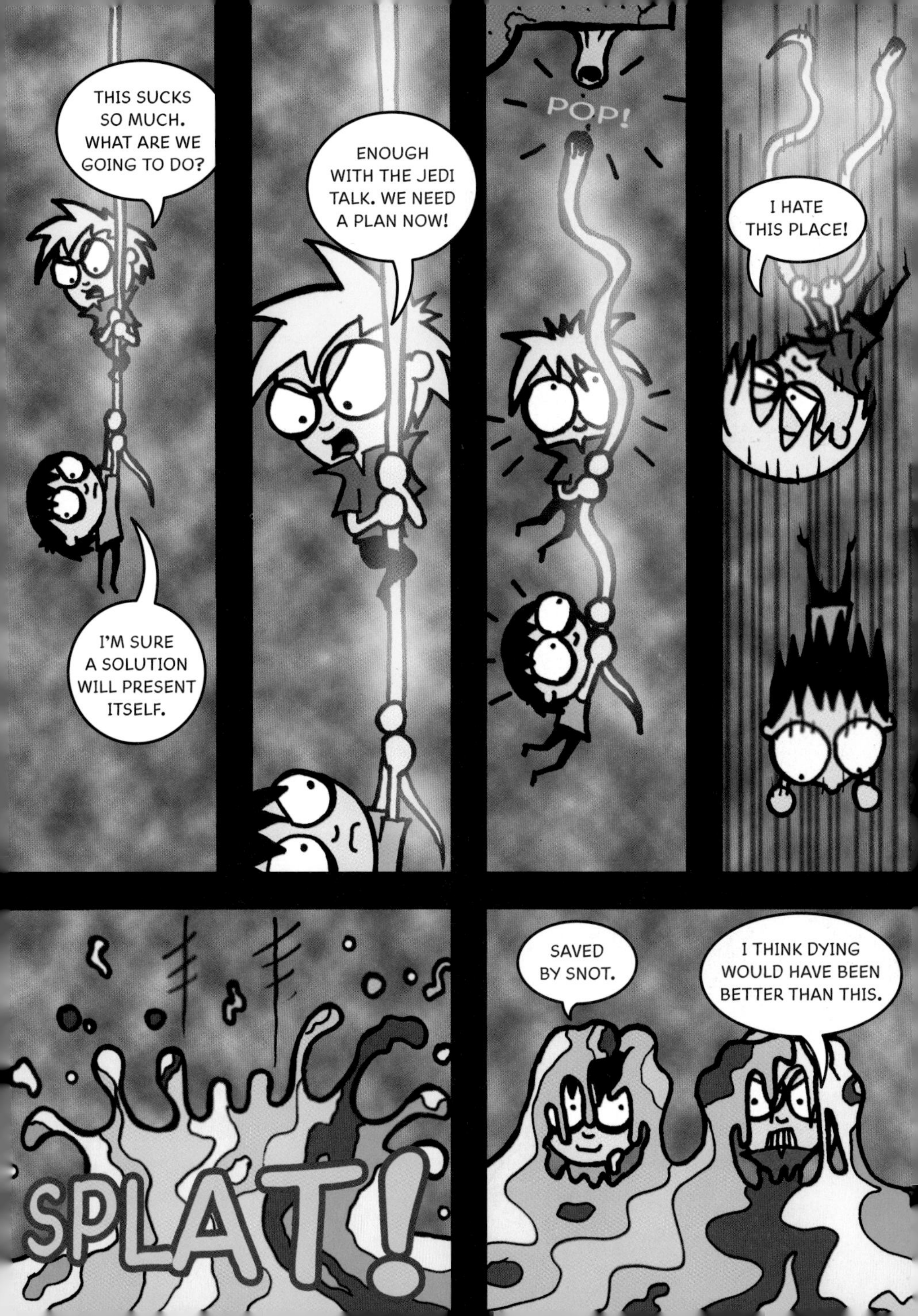
THIS SUCKS SO MUCH. WHAT ARE WE GOING TO DO?
I'M SURE A SOLUTION WILL PRESENT ITSELF.
ENOUGH WITH THE JEDI TALK. WE NEED A PLAN NOW!
POP!
I HATE THIS PLACE!
SPLAT!
SAVED BY SNOT.
I THINK DYING WOULD HAVE BEEN BETTER THAN THIS.

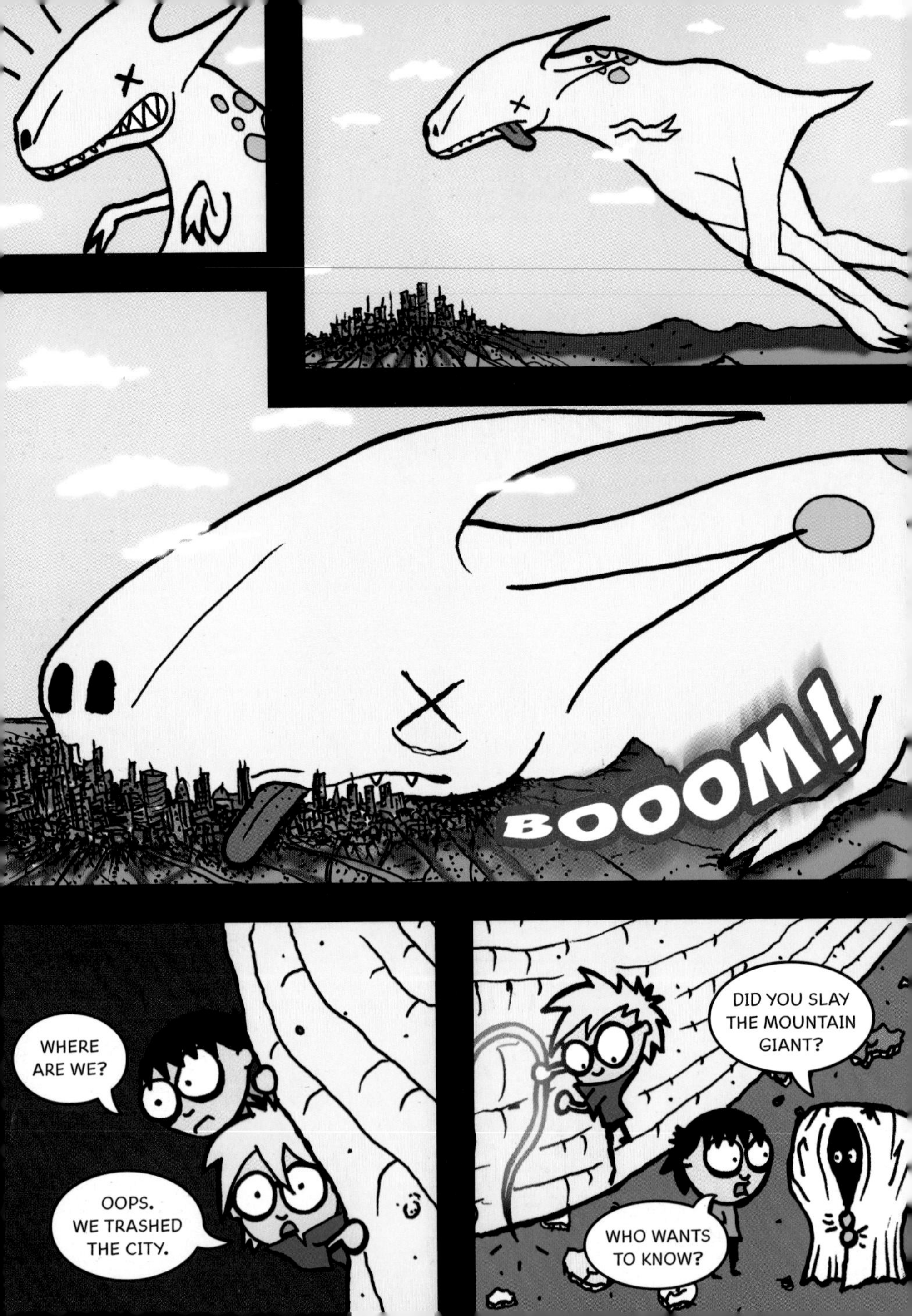
BOOOM!
WHERE ARE WE?
OOPS. WE TRASHED THE CITY.
DID YOU SLAY THE MOUNTAIN GIANT?
WHO WANTS TO KNOW?

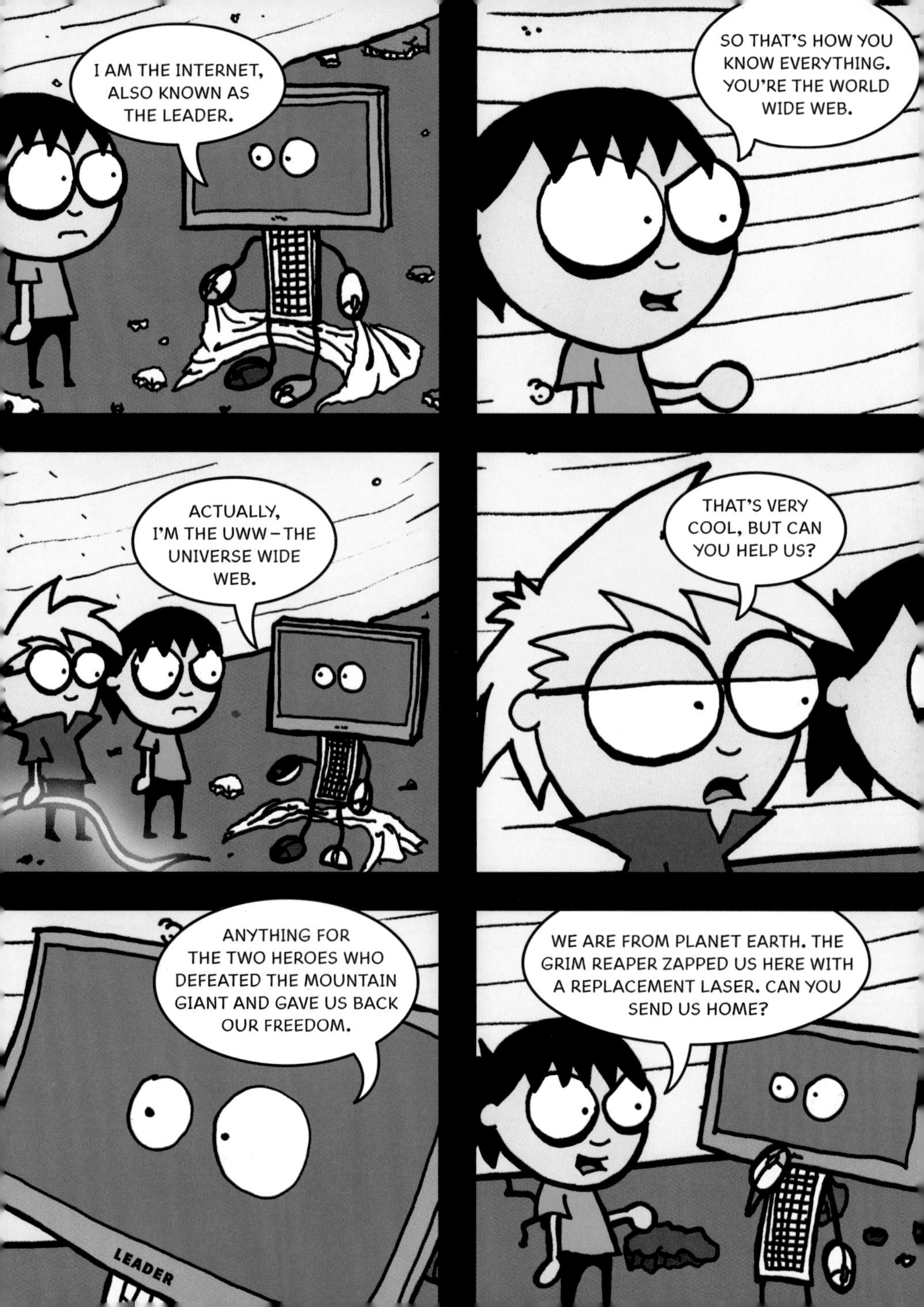
I AM THE INTERNET, ALSO KNOWN AS THE LEADER.
SO THAT'S HOW YOU KNOW EVERYTHING. YOU'RE THE WORLD WIDE WEB.
ACTUALLY, I'M THE UWW – THE UNIVERSE WIDE WEB.
THAT'S VERY COOL, BUT CAN YOU HELP US?
ANYTHING FOR THE TWO HEROES WHO DEFEATED THE MOUNTAIN GIANT AND GAVE US BACK OUR FREEDOM.
LEADER
WE ARE FROM PLANET EARTH. THE GRIM REAPER ZAPPED US HERE WITH A REPLACEMENT LASER. CAN YOU SEND US HOME?

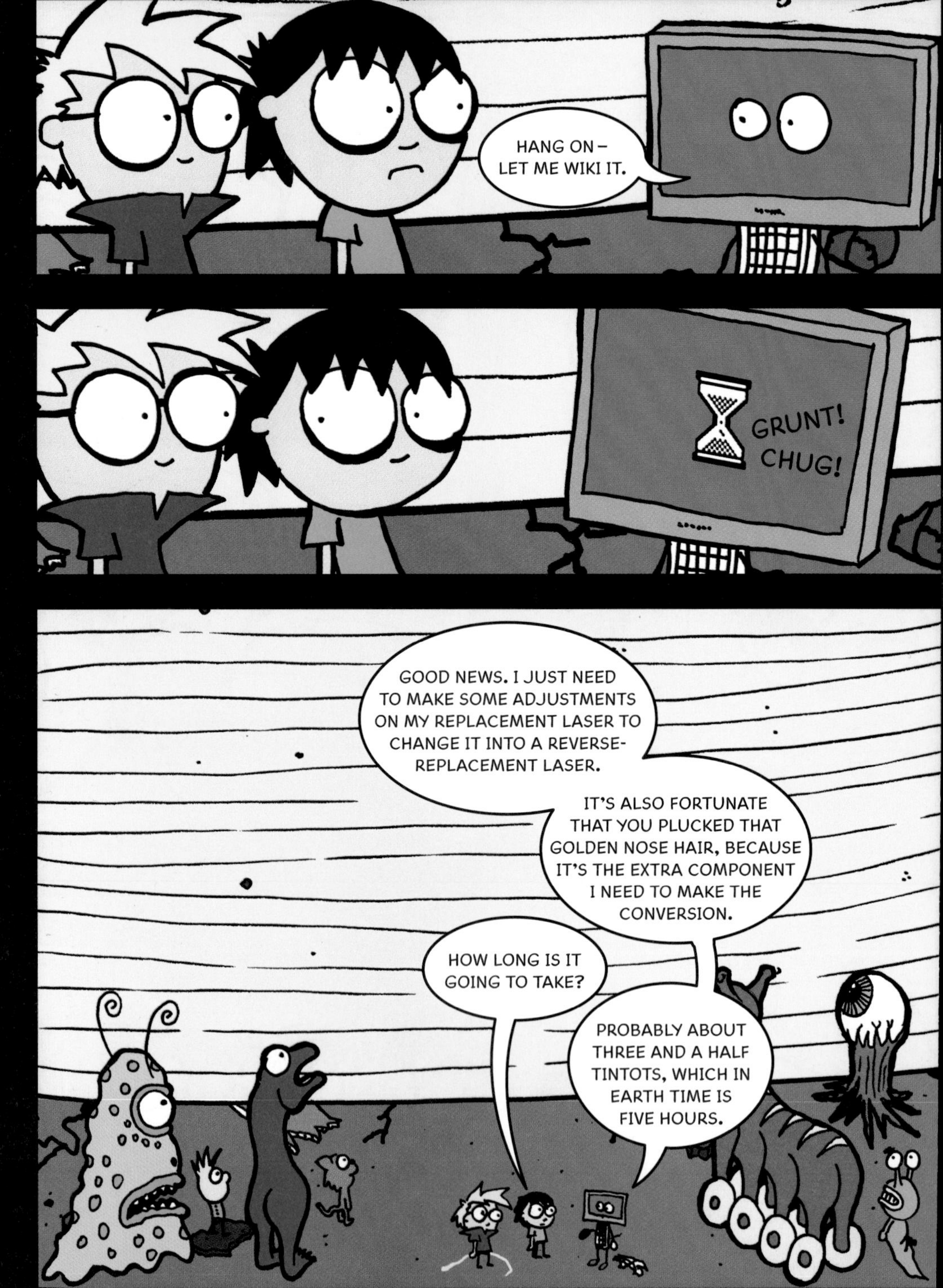
HANG ON—
LET ME WIKI IT.
GRUNT!
CHUG!
GOOD NEWS. I JUST NEED TO MAKE SOME ADJUSTMENTS ON MY REPLACEMENT LASER TO CHANGE IT INTO A REVERSE-REPLACEMENT LASER.
IT'S ALSO FORTUNATE THAT YOU PLUCKED THAT GOLDEN NOSE HAIR, BECAUSE IT'S THE EXTRA COMPONENT I NEED TO MAKE THE CONVERSION.
HOW LONG IS IT GOING TO TAKE?
PROBABLY ABOUT THREE AND A HALF TINTOTS, WHICH IN EARTH TIME IS FIVE HOURS.

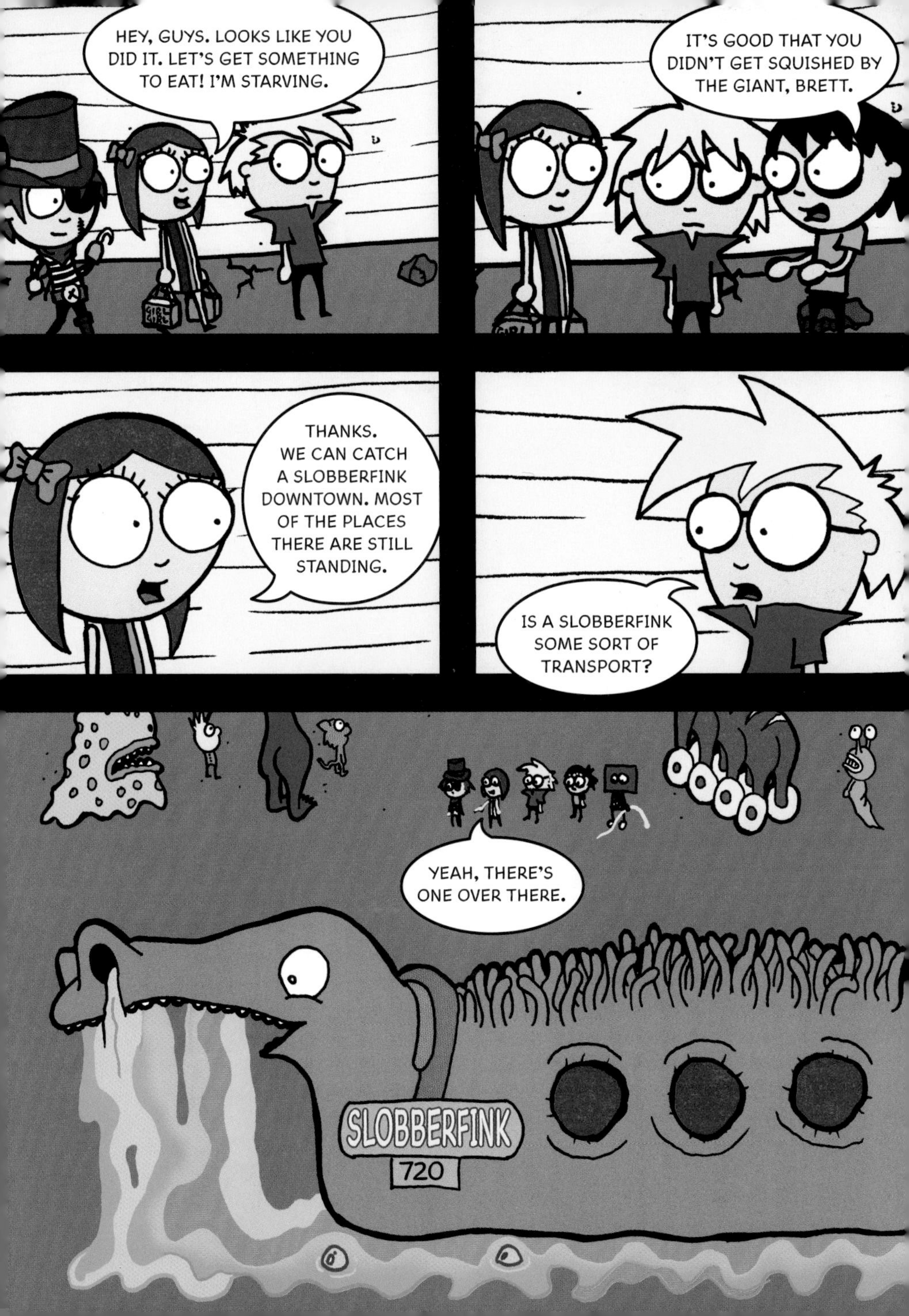
HEY, GUYS. LOOKS LIKE YOU DID IT. LET'S GET SOMETHING TO EAT! I'M STARVING.
IT'S GOOD THAT YOU DIDN'T GET SQUISHED BY THE GIANT, BRETT.
THANKS. WE CAN CATCH A SLOBBERFINK DOWNTOWN. MOST OF THE PLACES THERE ARE STILL STANDING.
IS A SLOBBERFINK SOME SORT OF TRANSPORT?
YEAH, THERE'S ONE OVER THERE.
SLOBBERFINK
720

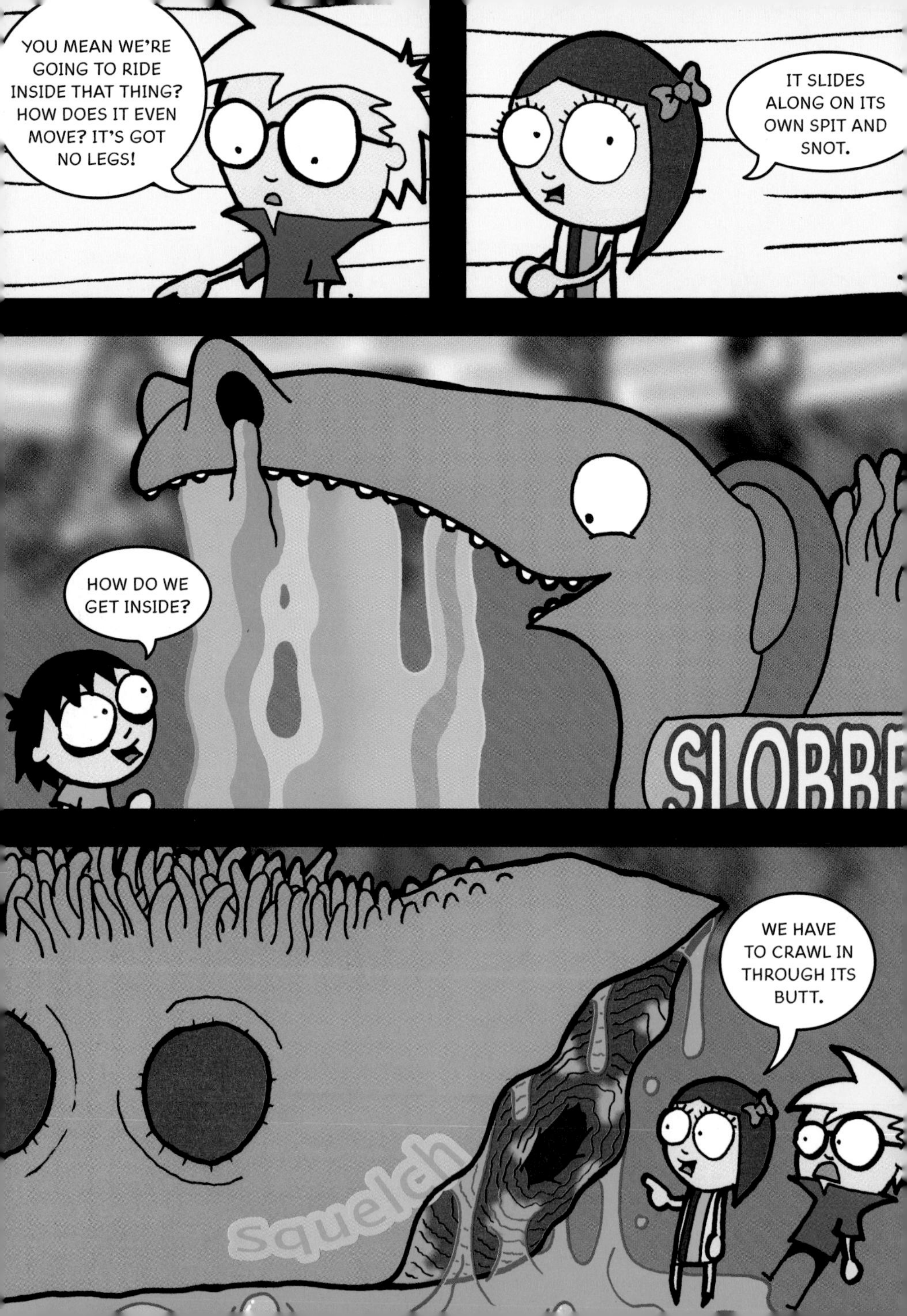
YOU MEAN WE'RE GOING TO RIDE INSIDE THAT THING? HOW DOES IT EVEN MOVE? IT'S GOT NO LEGS!
IT SLIDES ALONG ON ITS OWN SPIT AND SNOT.
HOW DO WE GET INSIDE?
SLOBBE
WE HAVE TO CRAWL IN THROUGH ITS BUTT.
Squelch

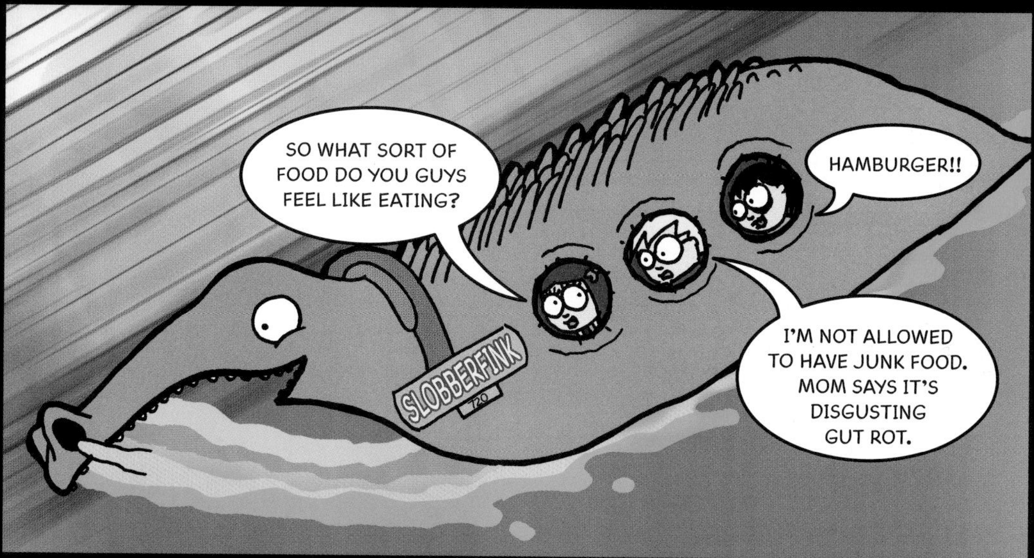
SO WHAT SORT OF FOOD DO YOU GUYS FEEL LIKE EATING?
HAMBURGER!!
I'M NOT ALLOWED TO HAVE JUNK FOOD. MOM SAYS IT'S DISGUSTING GUT ROT.
SLOBBERFINK
720

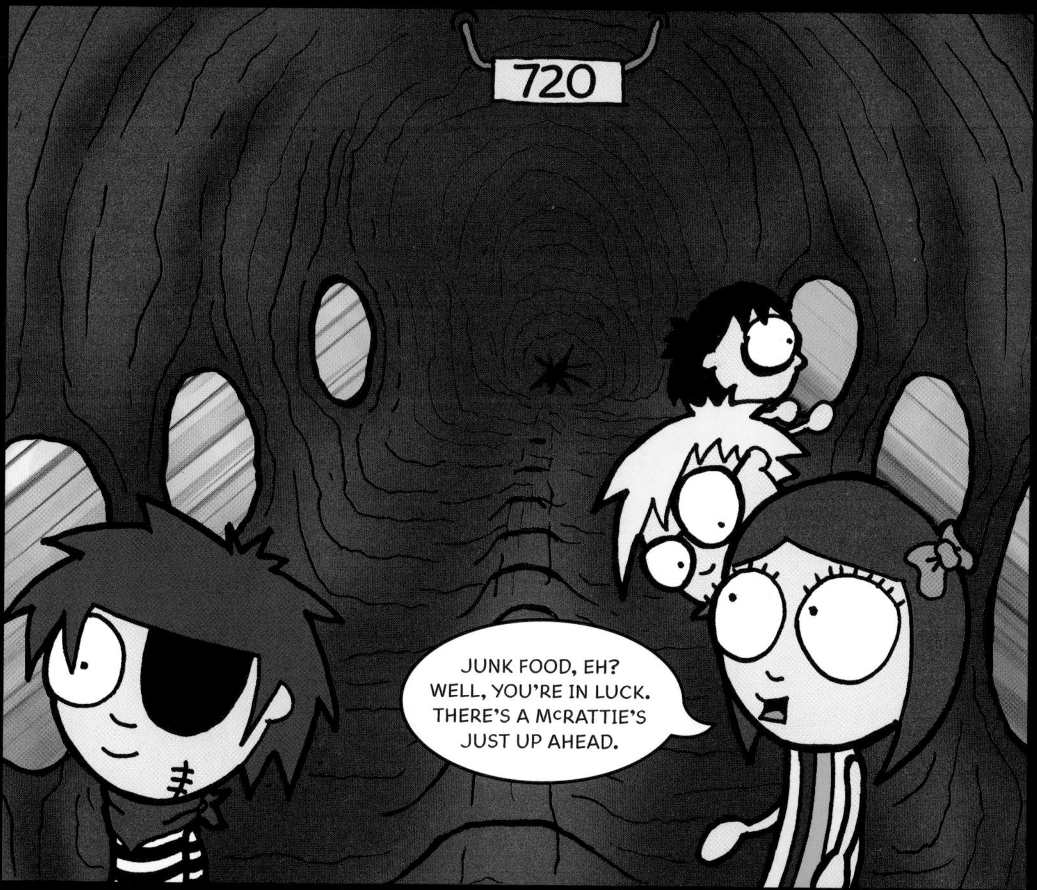
720
JUNK FOOD, EH? WELL, YOU'RE IN LUCK. THERE'S A McRATTIE'S JUST UP AHEAD.

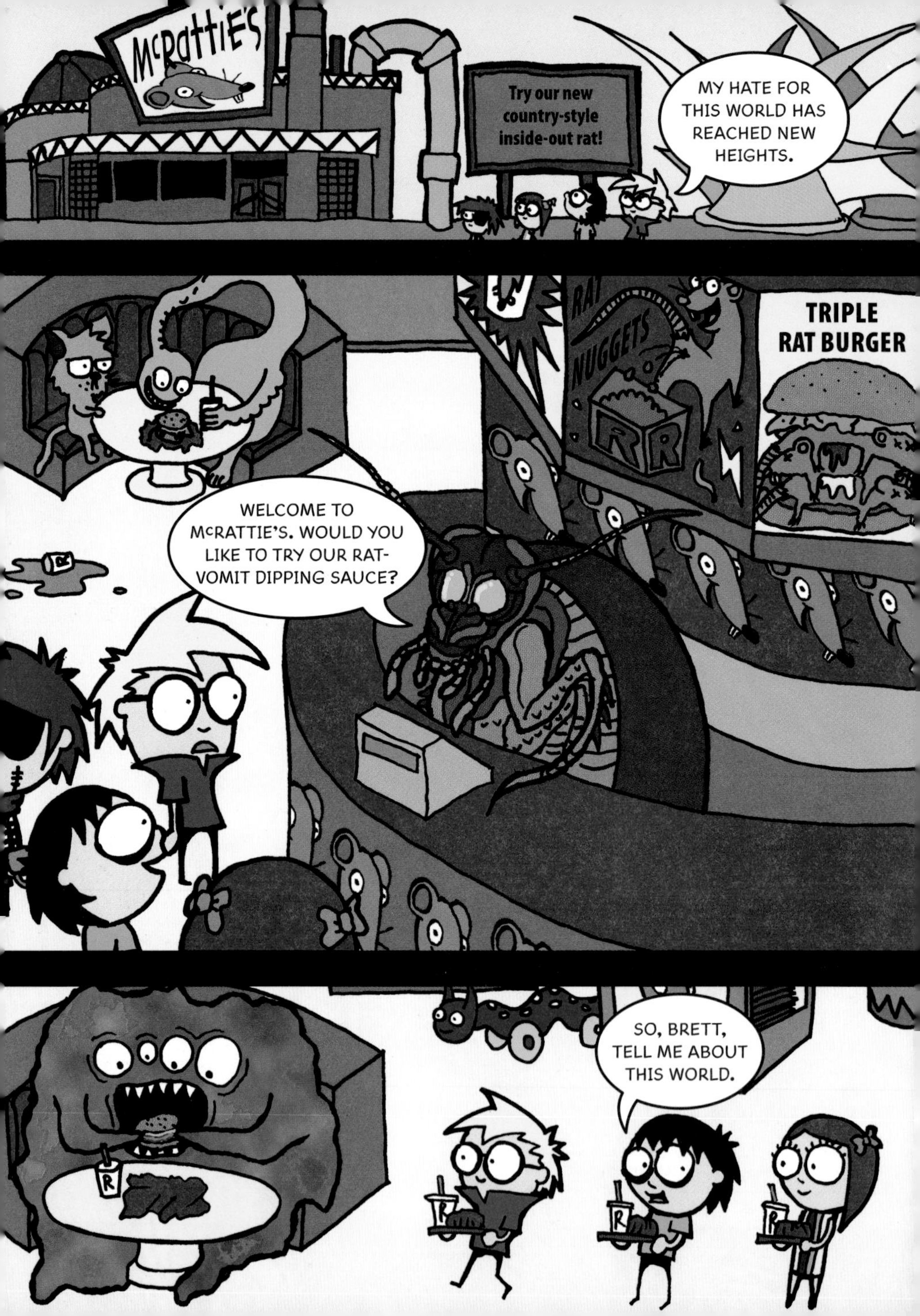

McRattie's
Try our new country-style inside-out rat!
MY HATE FOR THIS WORLD HAS REACHED NEW HEIGHTS.
RAT NUGGETS
TRIPLE RAT BURGER
WELCOME TO McRATTIE'S. WOULD YOU LIKE TO TRY OUR RAT-VOMIT DIPPING SAUCE?
SO, BRETT, TELL ME ABOUT THIS WORLD.

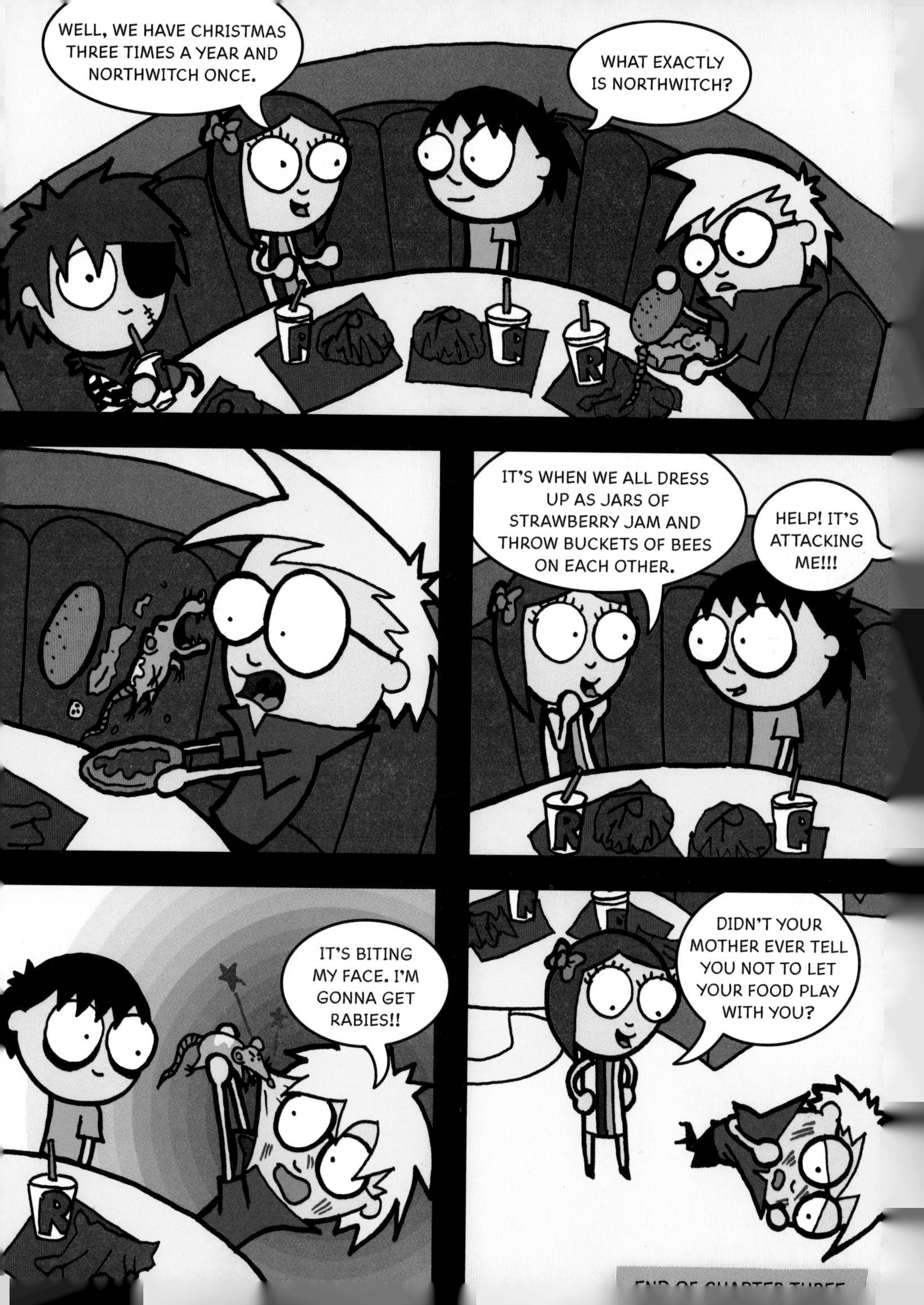
WELL, WE HAVE CHRISTMAS THREE TIMES A YEAR AND NORTHWITCH ONCE.
WHAT EXACTLY IS NORTHWITCH?
IT'S WHEN WE ALL DRESS UP AS JARS OF STRAWBERRY JAM AND THROW BUCKETS OF BEES ON EACH OTHER.
HELP! IT'S ATTACKING ME!!!
IT'S BITING MY FACE. I'M GONNA GET RABIES!!
DIDN'T YOUR MOTHER EVER TELL YOU NOT TO LET YOUR FOOD PLAY WITH YOU?

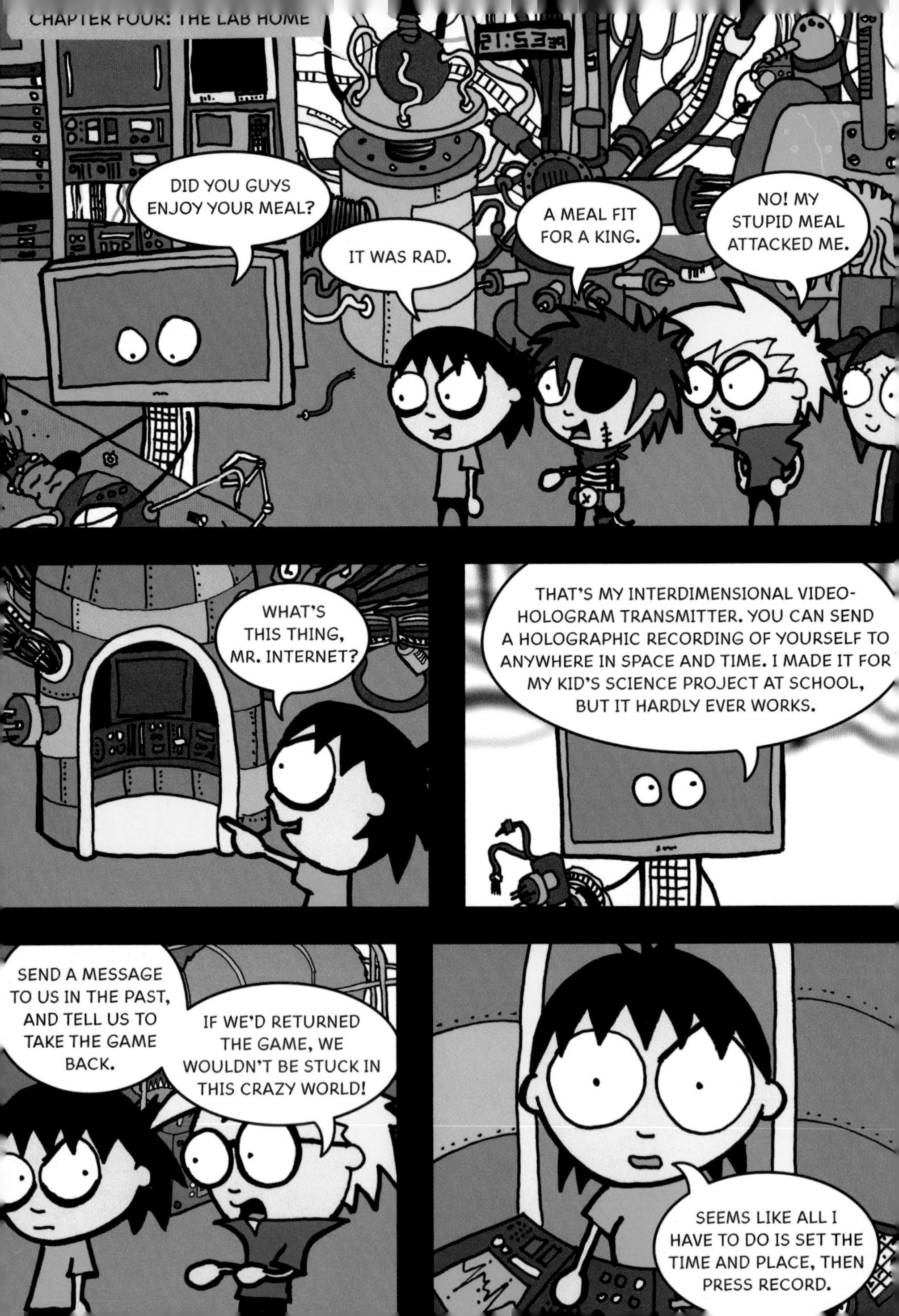
21:53
DID YOU GUYS ENJOY YOUR MEAL?
IT WAS RAD.
A MEAL FIT FOR A KING.
NO! MY STUPID MEAL ATTACKED ME.
WHAT'S THIS THING, MR. INTERNET?
THAT'S MY INTERDIMENSIONAL VIDEO-HOLOGRAM TRANSMITTER. YOU CAN SEND A HOLOGRAPHIC RECORDING OF YOURSELF TO ANYWHERE IN SPACE AND TIME. I MADE IT FOR MY KID'S SCIENCE PROJECT AT SCHOOL, BUT IT HARDLY EVER WORKS.
SEND A MESSAGE TO US IN THE PAST, AND TELL US TO TAKE THE GAME BACK.
IF WE'D RETURNED THE GAME, WE WOULDN'T BE STUCK IN THIS CRAZY WORLD!
SEEMS LIKE ALL I HAVE TO DO IS SET THE TIME AND PLACE, THEN PRESS RECORD.

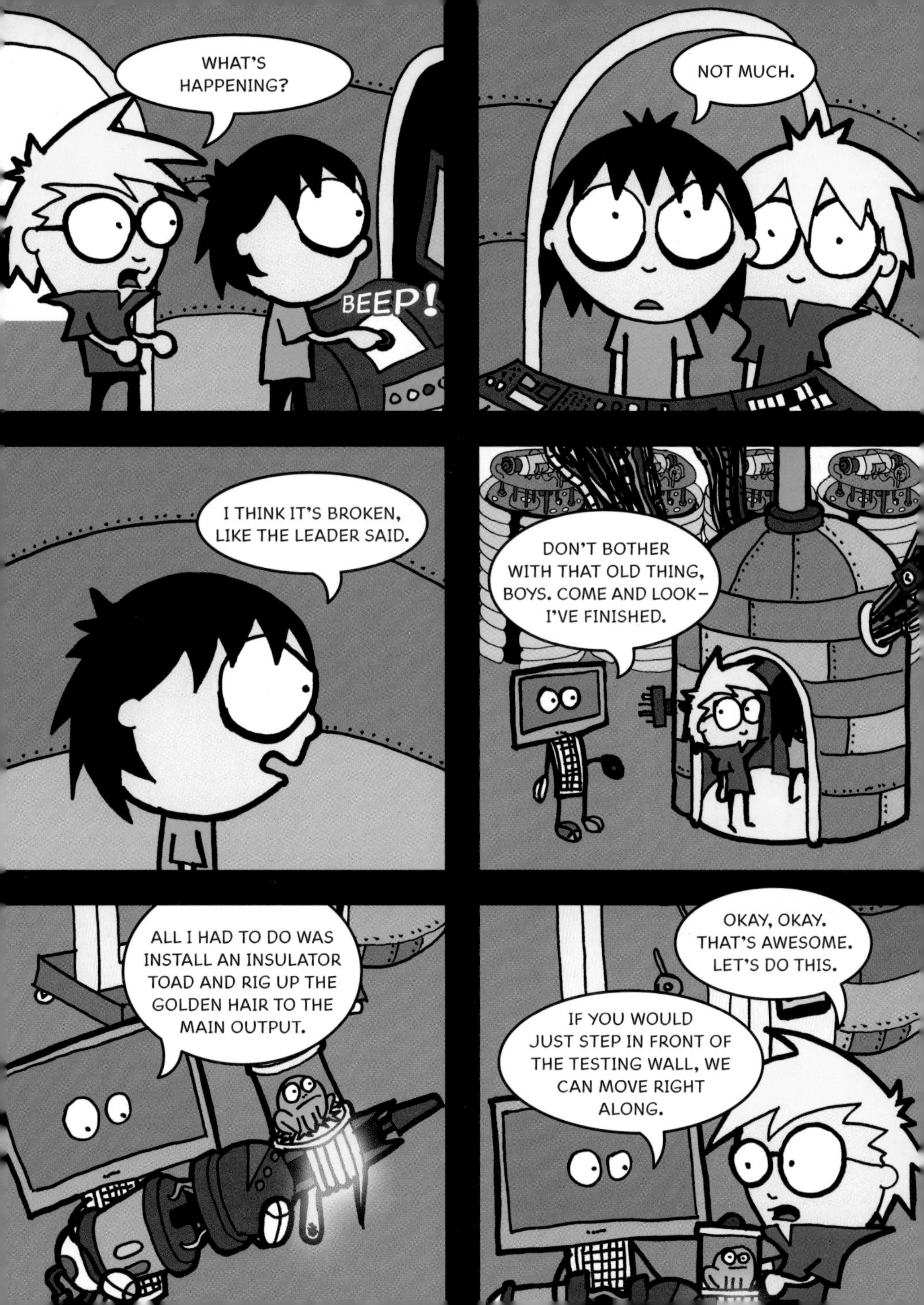
WHAT'S HAPPENING?
BEEP!
NOT MUCH.
I THINK IT'S BROKEN, LIKE THE LEADER SAID.
DON'T BOTHER WITH THAT OLD THING, BOYS. COME AND LOOK– I'VE FINISHED.
ALL I HAD TO DO WAS INSTALL AN INSULATOR TOAD AND RIG UP THE GOLDEN HAIR TO THE MAIN OUTPUT.
OKAY, OKAY. THAT'S AWESOME. LET'S DO THIS.
IF YOU WOULD JUST STEP IN FRONT OF THE TESTING WALL, WE CAN MOVE RIGHT ALONG.

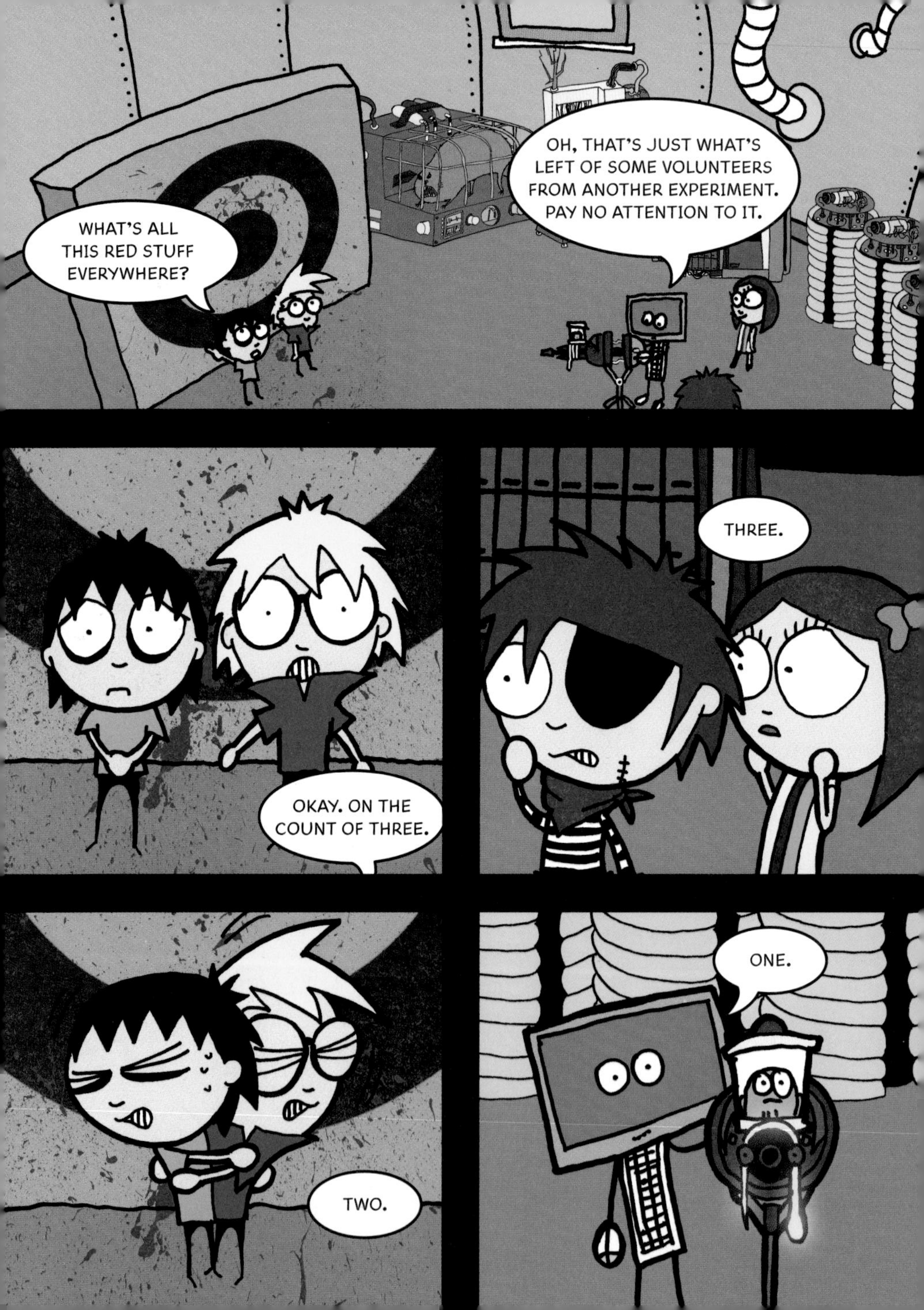
WHAT'S ALL THIS RED STUFF EVERYWHERE?
OH, THAT'S JUST WHAT'S LEFT OF SOME VOLUNTEERS FROM ANOTHER EXPERIMENT. PAY NO ATTENTION TO IT.
OKAY. ON THE COUNT OF THREE.
THREE.
TWO.
ONE.

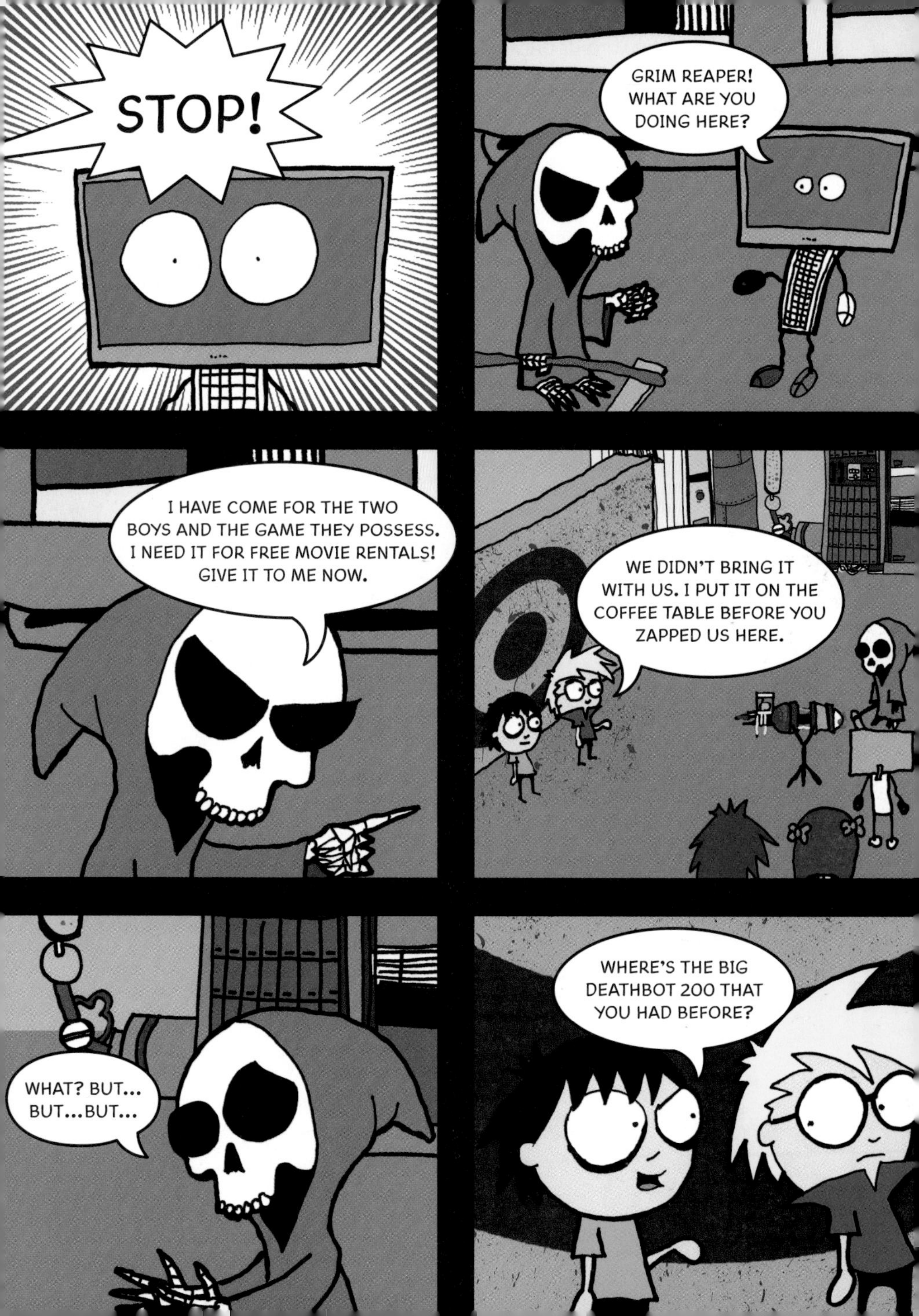
STOP!
GRIM REAPER! WHAT ARE YOU DOING HERE?
I HAVE COME FOR THE TWO BOYS AND THE GAME THEY POSSESS. I NEED IT FOR FREE MOVIE RENTALS! GIVE IT TO ME NOW.
WE DIDN'T BRING IT WITH US. I PUT IT ON THE COFFEE TABLE BEFORE YOU ZAPPED US HERE.
WHAT? BUT... BUT...BUT...
WHERE'S THE BIG DEATHBOT 200 THAT YOU HAD BEFORE?

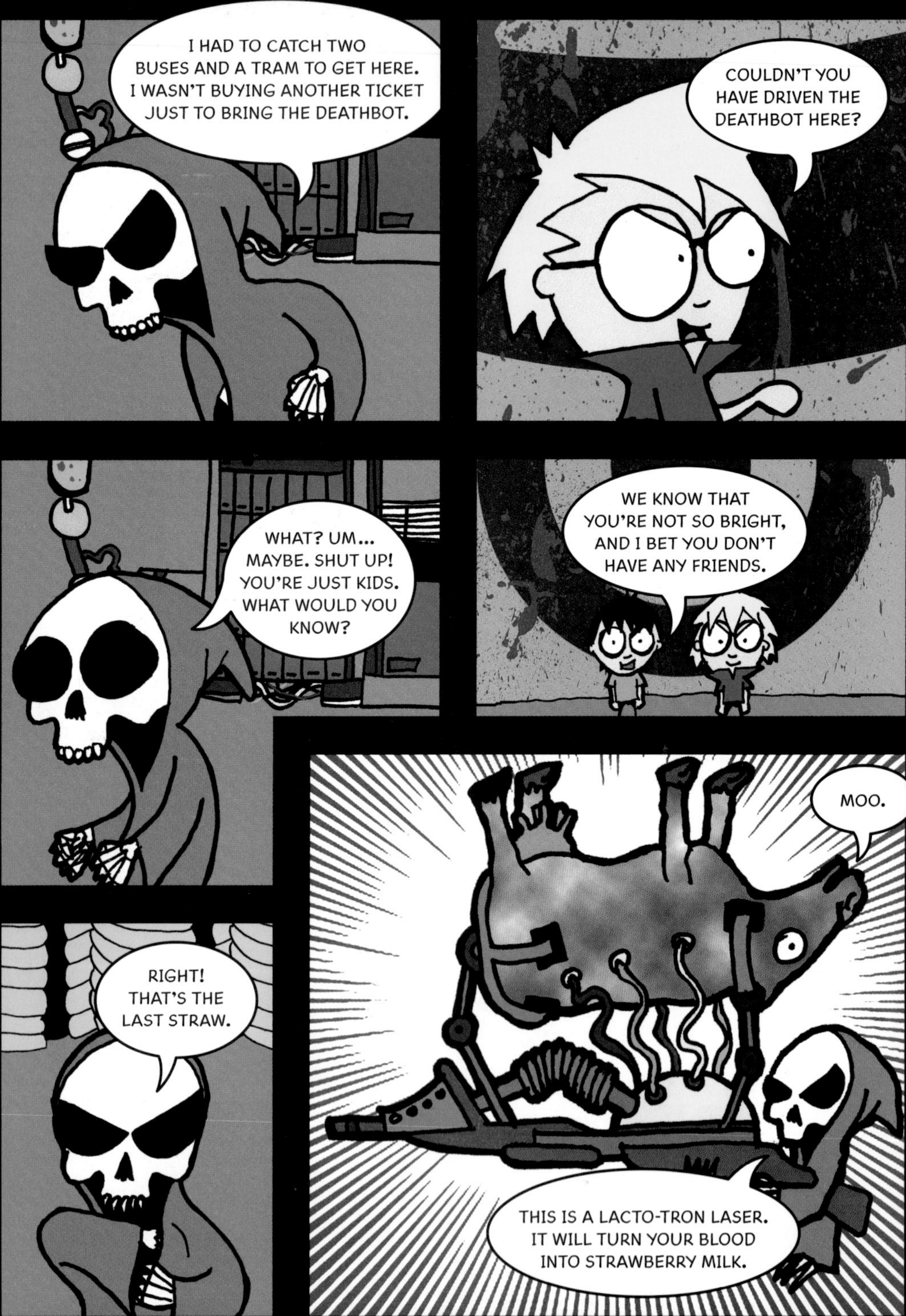
I HAD TO CATCH TWO BUSES AND A TRAM TO GET HERE. I WASN'T BUYING ANOTHER TICKET JUST TO BRING THE DEATHBOT.
COULDN'T YOU HAVE DRIVEN THE DEATHBOT HERE?
WHAT? UM... MAYBE. SHUT UP! YOU'RE JUST KIDS. WHAT WOULD YOU KNOW?
WE KNOW THAT YOU'RE NOT SO BRIGHT, AND I BET YOU DON'T HAVE ANY FRIENDS.
RIGHT! THAT'S THE LAST STRAW.
MOO.
THIS IS A LACTO-TRON LASER. IT WILL TURN YOUR BLOOD INTO STRAWBERRY MILK.

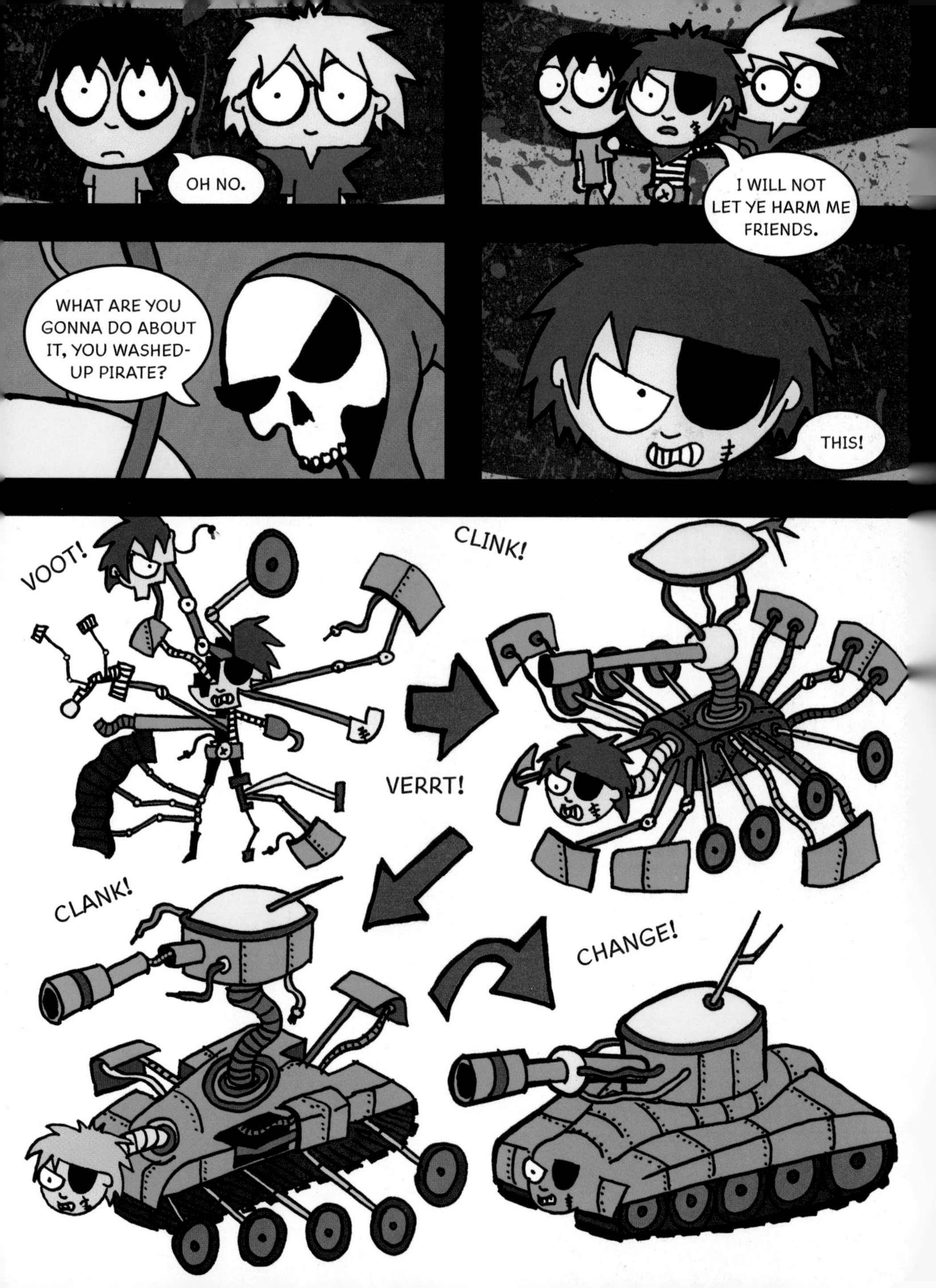
OH NO.
I WILL NOT LET YE HARM ME FRIENDS.
WHAT ARE YOU GONNA DO ABOUT IT, YOU WASHED-UP PIRATE?
THIS!
VOOT!
CLINK!
VERRT!
CLANK!
CHANGE!

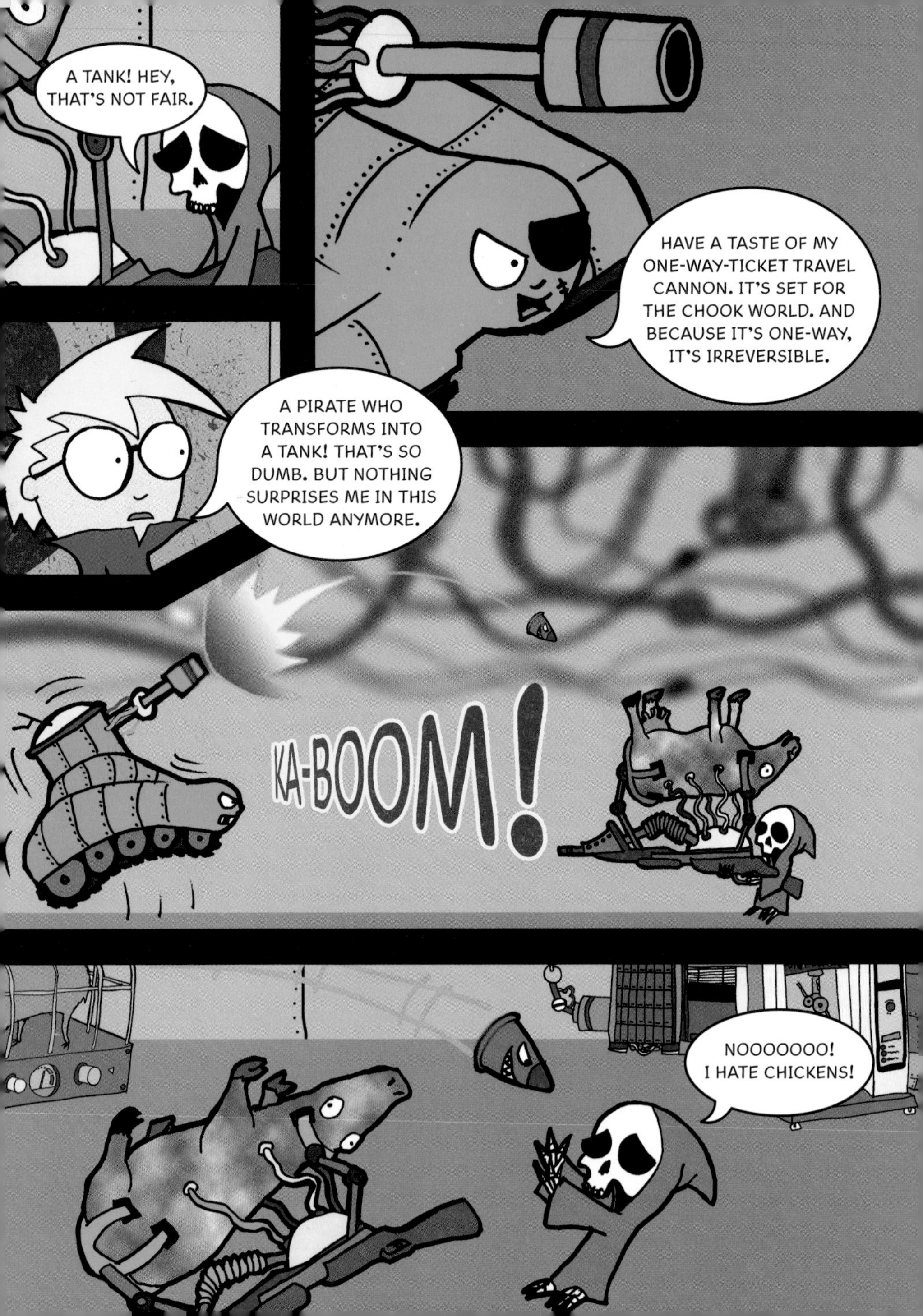
A TANK! HEY, THAT'S NOT FAIR.
HAVE A TASTE OF MY ONE-WAY-TICKET TRAVEL CANNON. IT'S SET FOR THE CHOOK WORLD. AND BECAUSE IT'S ONE-WAY, IT'S IRREVERSIBLE.
A PIRATE WHO TRANSFORMS INTO A TANK! THAT'S SO DUMB. BUT NOTHING SURPRISES ME IN THIS WORLD ANYMORE.
KA-BOOM!
NOOOOOOO! I HATE CHICKENS!

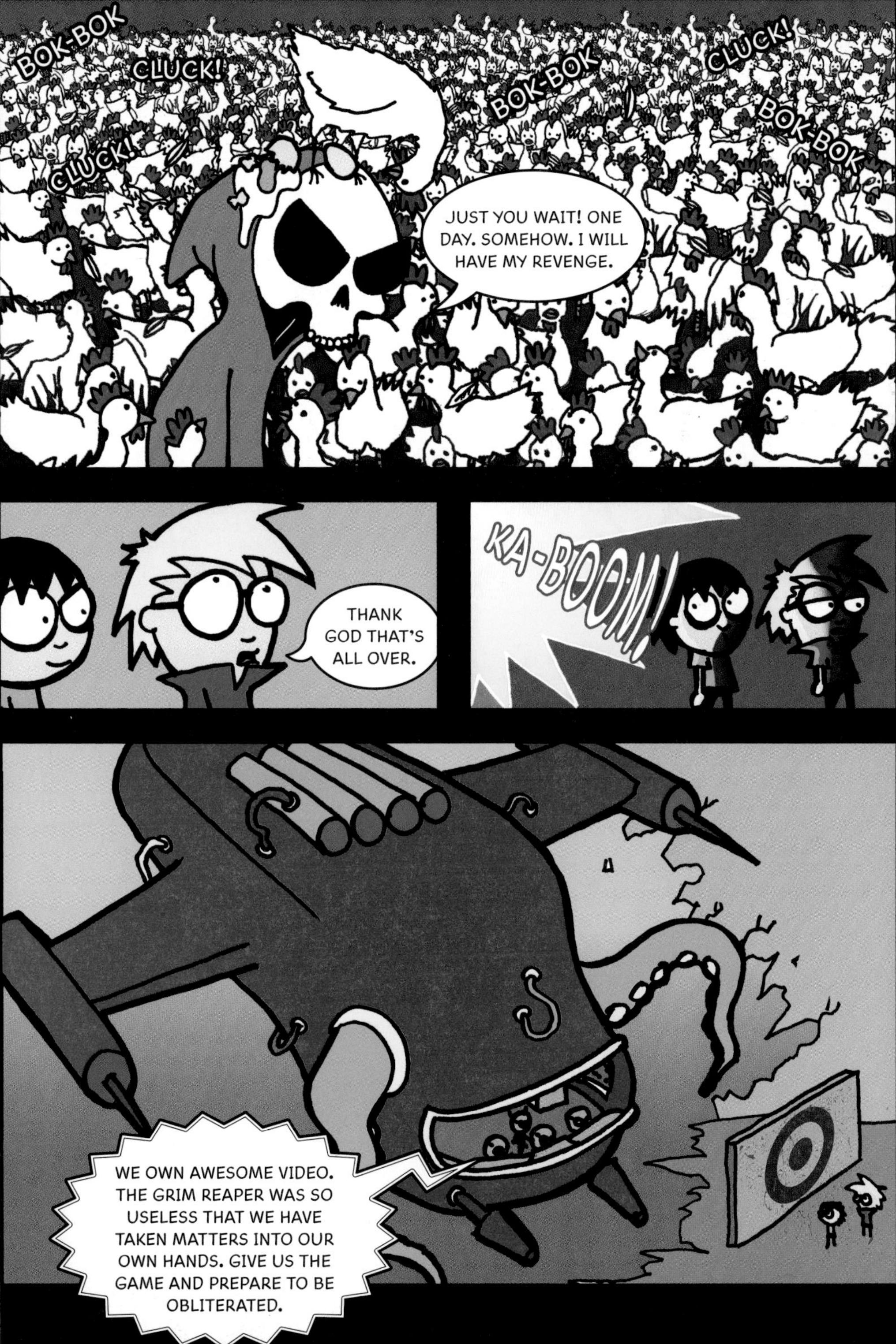
BOK-BOK
CLUCK!
CLUCK!
BOK-BOK
CLUCK!
BOK-BOK
JUST YOU WAIT! ONE DAY. SOMEHOW. I WILL HAVE MY REVENGE.
THANK GOD THAT'S ALL OVER.
KA-BOOM!
WE OWN AWESOME VIDEO. THE GRIM REAPER WAS SO USELESS THAT WE HAVE TAKEN MATTERS INTO OUR OWN HANDS. GIVE US THE GAME AND PREPARE TO BE OBLITERATED.

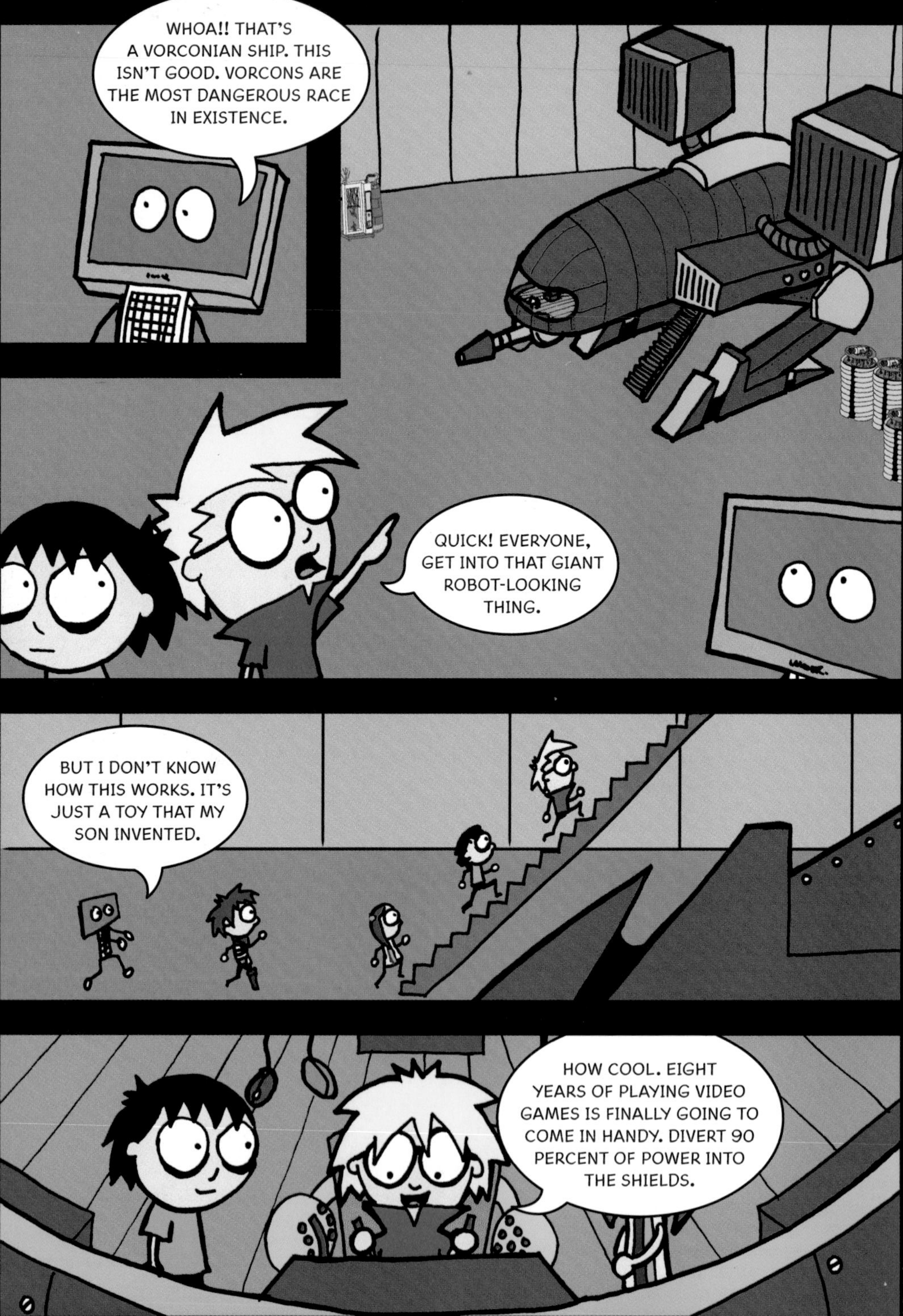
WHOA!! THAT'S A VORCONIAN SHIP. THIS ISN'T GOOD. VORCONS ARE THE MOST DANGEROUS RACE IN EXISTENCE.
QUICK! EVERYONE, GET INTO THAT GIANT ROBOT-LOOKING THING.
BUT I DON'T KNOW HOW THIS WORKS. IT'S JUST A TOY THAT MY SON INVENTED.
HOW COOL. EIGHT YEARS OF PLAYING VIDEO GAMES IS FINALLY GOING TO COME IN HANDY. DIVERT 90 PERCENT OF POWER INTO THE SHIELDS.

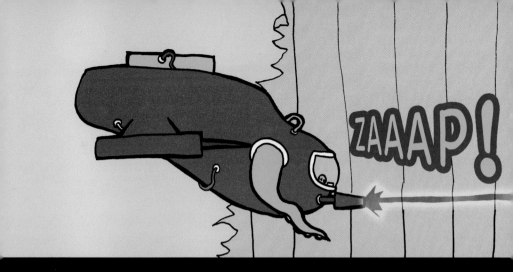

ZAAAP!

BWORR!

WAY TO GO, HUXLEY! NOW FIRE OUR LASERS AT THEM.

I CAN'T. THE SHIP'S COMPUTER SAYS THAT IT HAS NO WEAPONS.

BUT WHAT ABOUT THAT REALLY BIG GUN STICKING OUT THE FRONT?

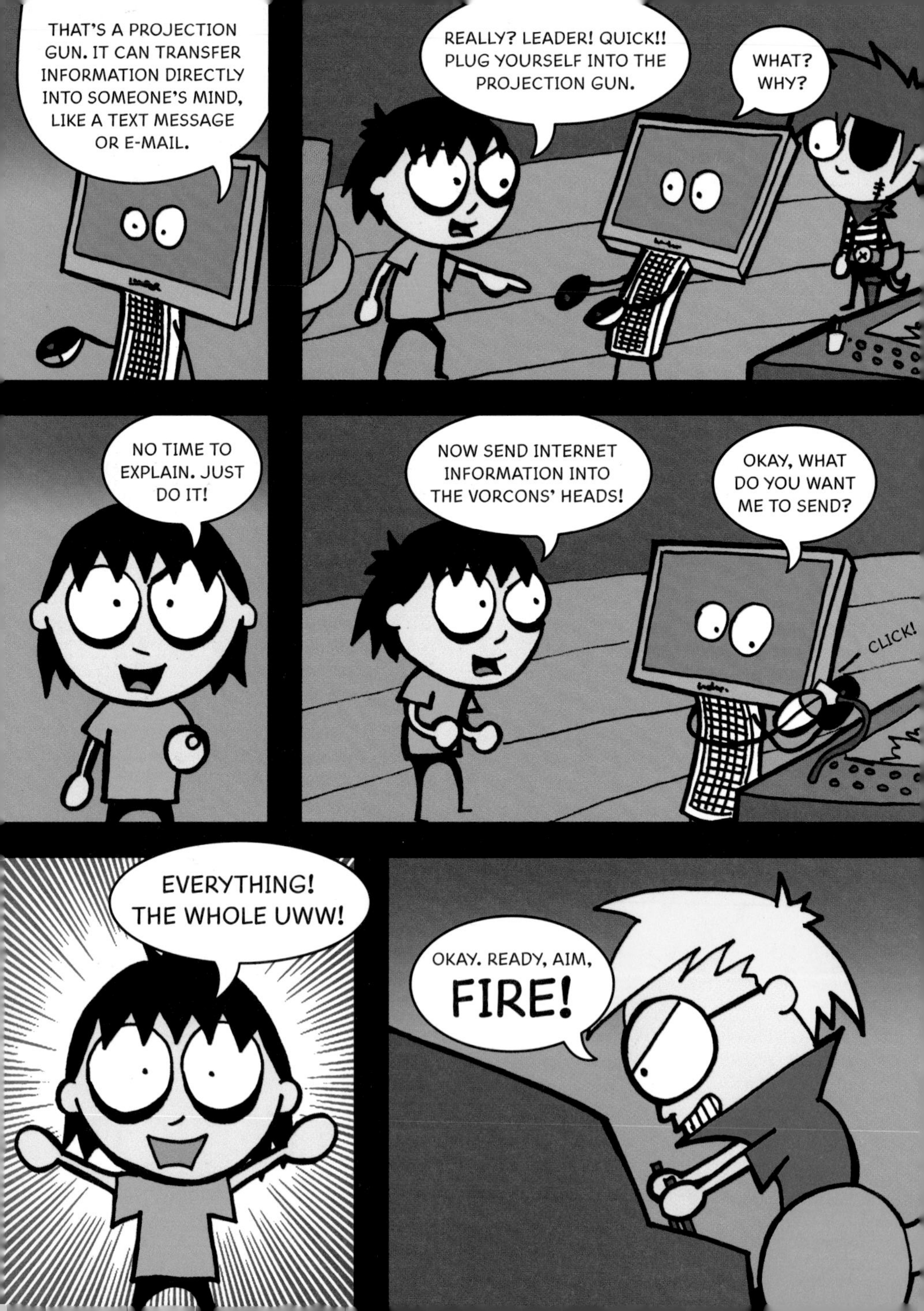
THAT'S A PROJECTION GUN. IT CAN TRANSFER INFORMATION DIRECTLY INTO SOMEONE'S MIND, LIKE A TEXT MESSAGE OR E-MAIL.
REALLY? LEADER! QUICK!! PLUG YOURSELF INTO THE PROJECTION GUN.
WHAT? WHY?
NO TIME TO EXPLAIN. JUST DO IT!
NOW SEND INTERNET INFORMATION INTO THE VORCONS' HEADS!
OKAY, WHAT DO YOU WANT ME TO SEND?
CLICK!
EVERYTHING! THE WHOLE UWW!
OKAY. READY, AIM,
FIRE!

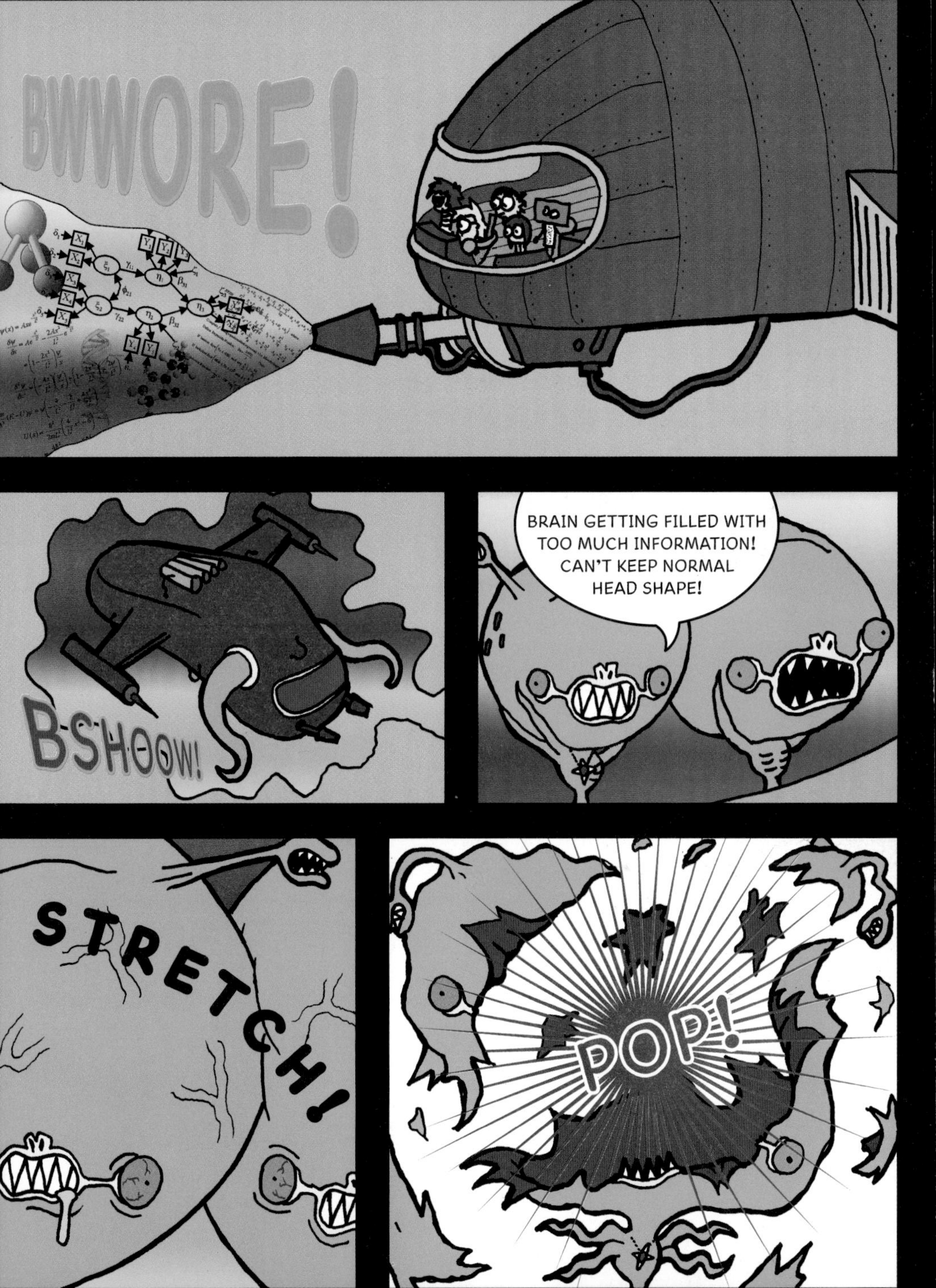
BWWORE!
B-SHOOW!
BRAIN GETTING FILLED WITH TOO MUCH INFORMATION! CAN'T KEEP NORMAL HEAD SHAPE!
STRETCH!
POP!

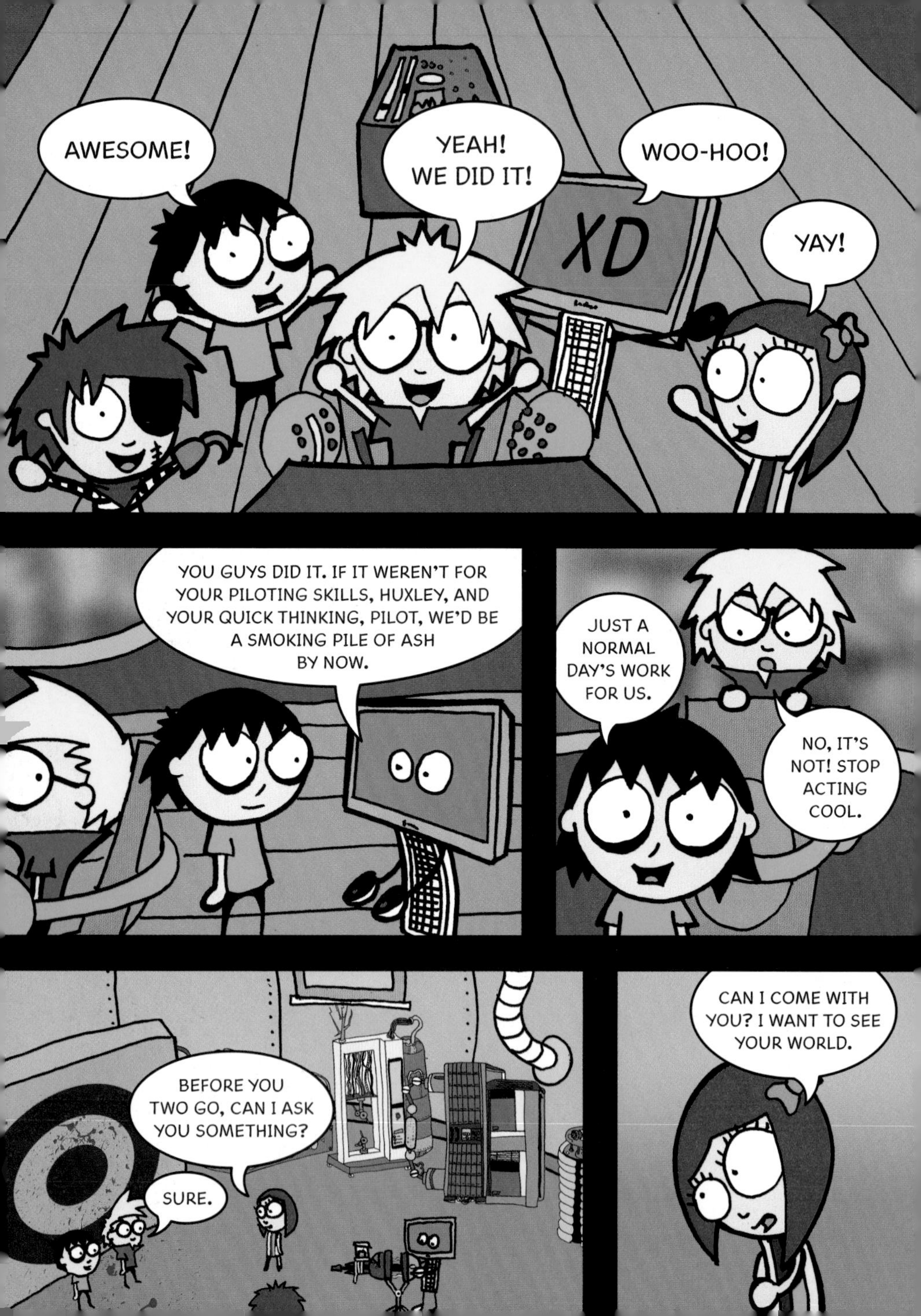
AWESOME!
YEAH! WE DID IT!
WOO-HOO!
XD
YAY!
YOU GUYS DID IT. IF IT WEREN'T FOR YOUR PILOTING SKILLS, HUXLEY, AND YOUR QUICK THINKING, PILOT, WE'D BE A SMOKING PILE OF ASH BY NOW.
JUST A NORMAL DAY'S WORK FOR US.
NO, IT'S NOT! STOP ACTING COOL.
BEFORE YOU TWO GO, CAN I ASK YOU SOMETHING?
SURE.
CAN I COME WITH YOU? I WANT TO SEE YOUR WORLD.

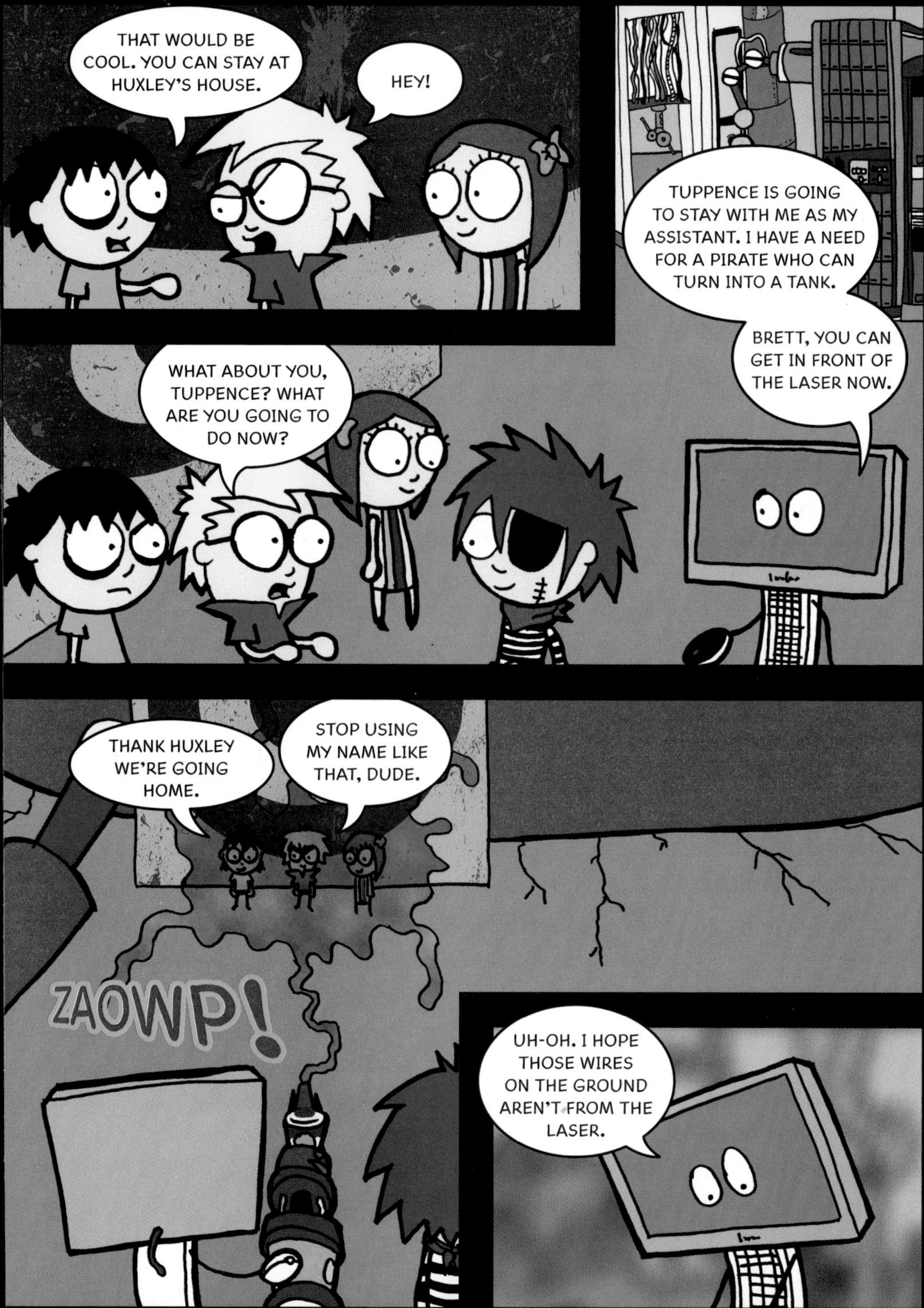
THAT WOULD BE COOL. YOU CAN STAY AT HUXLEY'S HOUSE.
HEY!
TUPPENCE IS GOING TO STAY WITH ME AS MY ASSISTANT. I HAVE A NEED FOR A PIRATE WHO CAN TURN INTO A TANK.
WHAT ABOUT YOU, TUPPENCE? WHAT ARE YOU GOING TO DO NOW?
BRETT, YOU CAN GET IN FRONT OF THE LASER NOW.
THANK HUXLEY WE'RE GOING HOME.
STOP USING MY NAME LIKE THAT, DUDE.
ZAOWP!
UH-OH. I HOPE THOSE WIRES ON THE GROUND AREN'T FROM THE LASER.

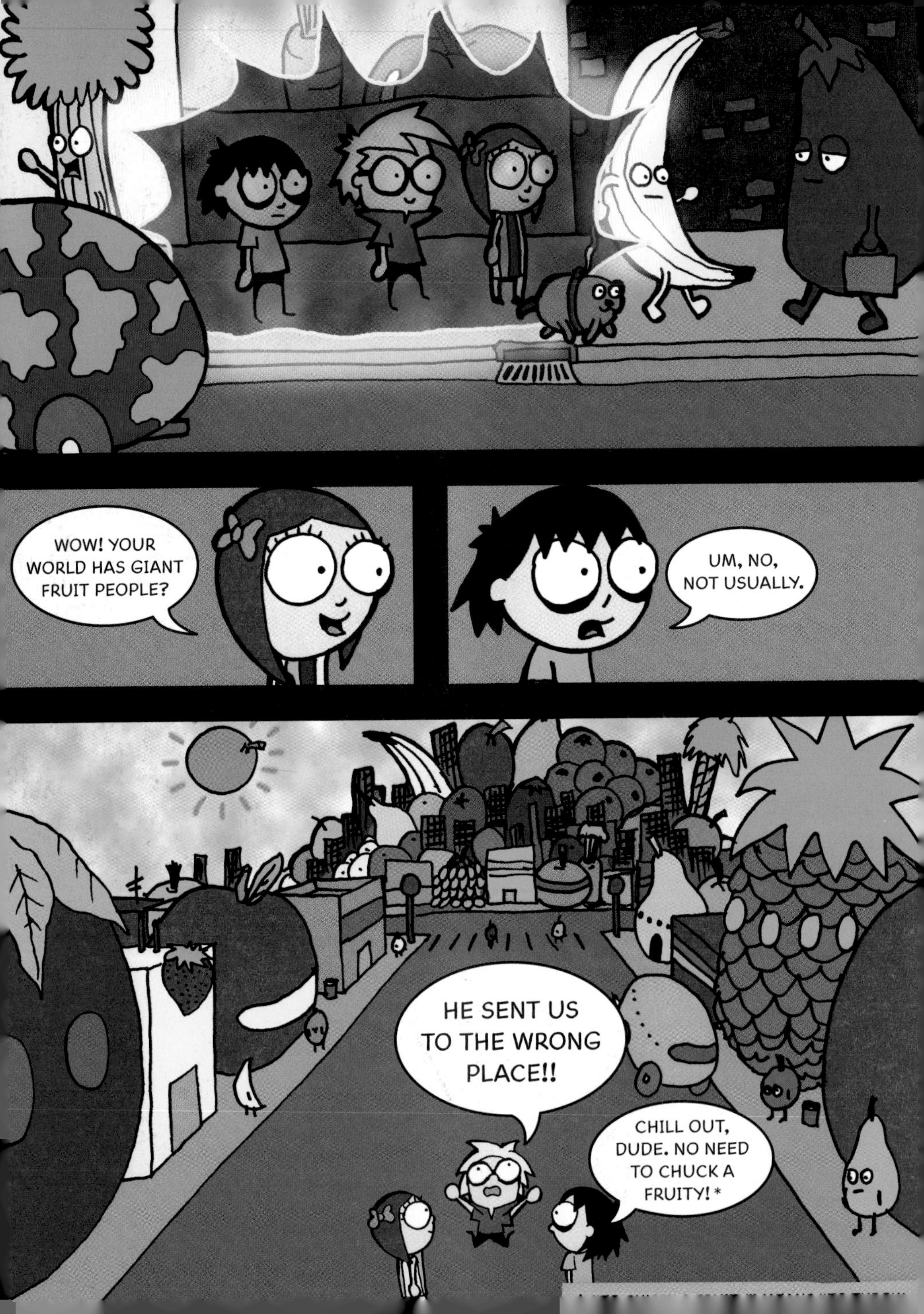
WOW! YOUR WORLD HAS GIANT FRUIT PEOPLE?
UM, NO, NOT USUALLY.
HE SENT US TO THE WRONG PLACE!!
CHILL OUT, DUDE. NO NEED TO CHUCK A FRUITY! *

AFTERWORD

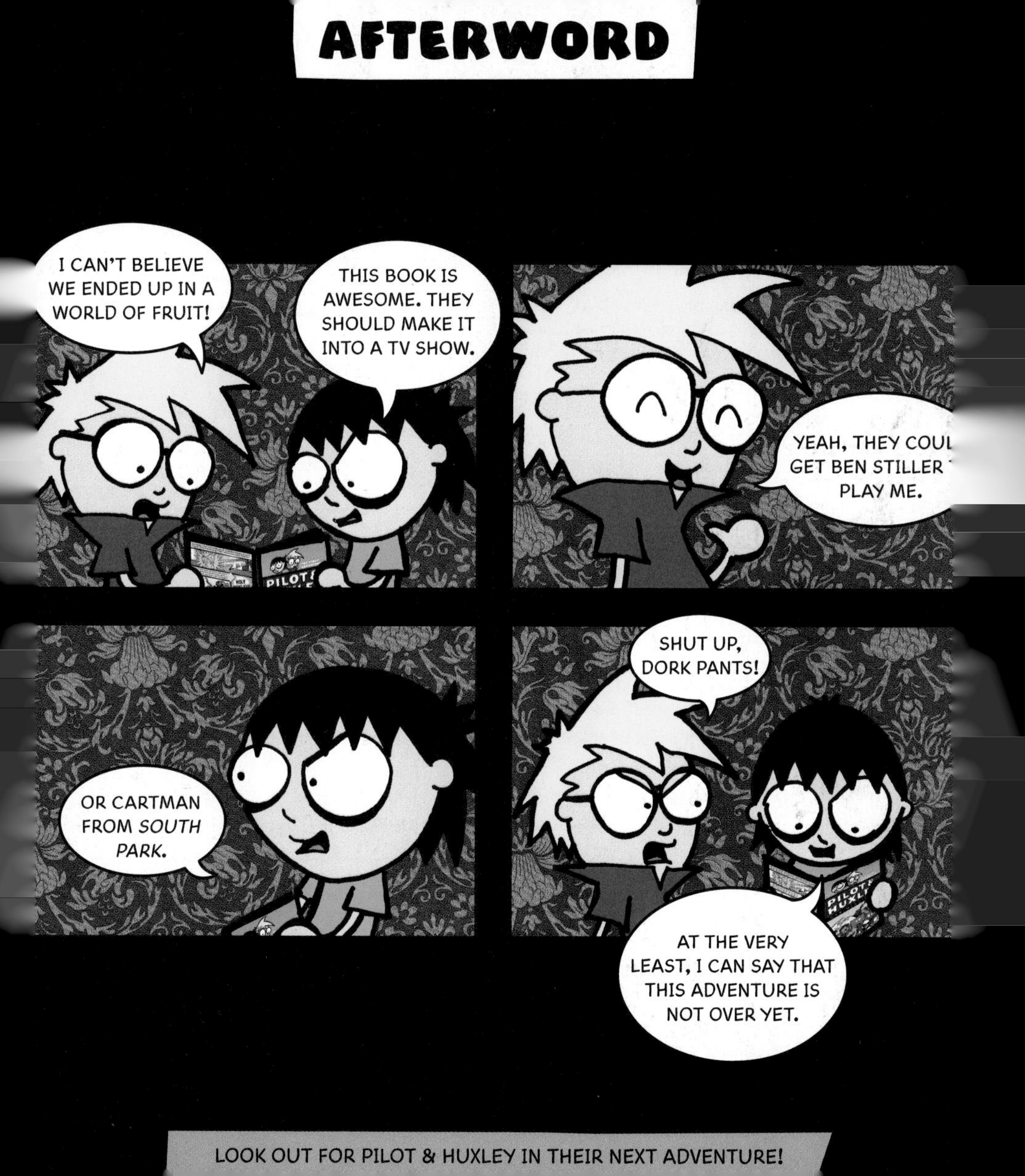
I CAN'T BELIEVE WE ENDED UP IN A WORLD OF FRUIT!
THIS BOOK IS AWESOME. THEY SHOULD MAKE IT INTO A TV SHOW.
PILOT
YEAH, THEY COUL GET BEN STILLER PLAY ME.
OR CARTMAN FROM *SOUTH PARK.*
SHUT UP, DORK PANTS!
AT THE VERY LEAST, I CAN SAY THAT THIS ADVENTURE IS NOT OVER YET.

LOOK OUT FOR PILOT & HUXLEY IN THEIR NEXT ADVENTURE!

ABOUT THE AUTHOR

DAN McGUINESS WAS DISCOVERED AS AN INFANT AMONG THE SMOLDERING REMAINS OF A TOP SECRET LABORATORY.

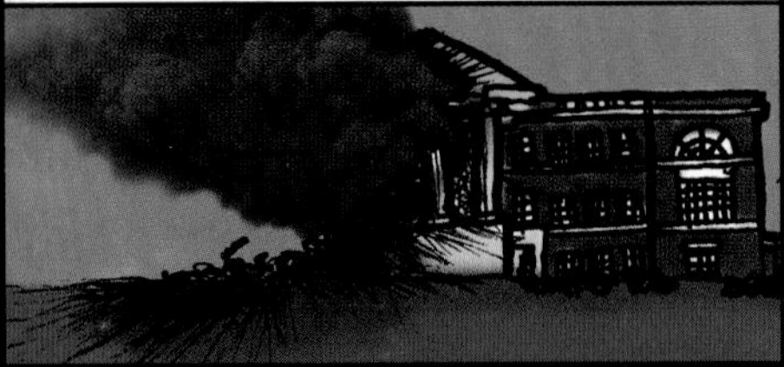

HE GREW UP UNDER CLOSE SCRUTINY IN A MILITARY FACILITY OF UNCERTAIN LOCATION.

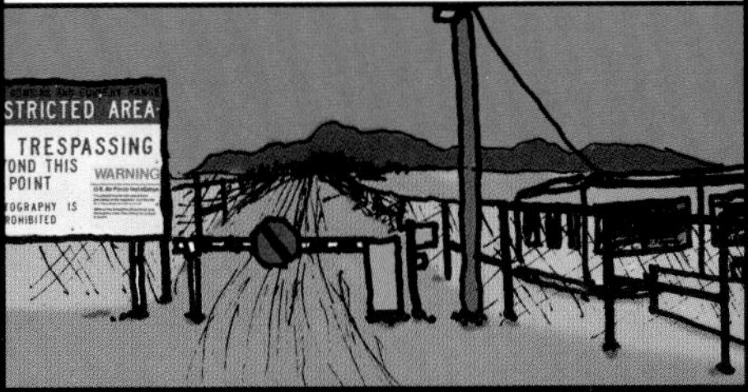
TRESPASSING
POINT
WARNING

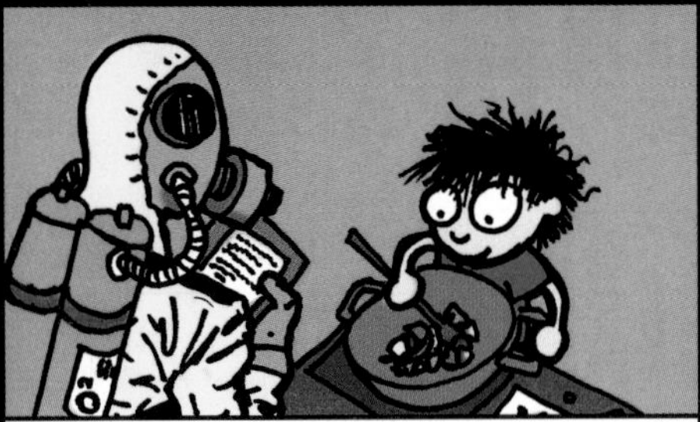

THE ARMY'S TOP SCIENTISTS ATTEMPTED TO HARNESS HIS EXTRAORDINARY POWERS OF STIR-FRY COOKERY AND REACHING THINGS ON HIGH SHELVES.

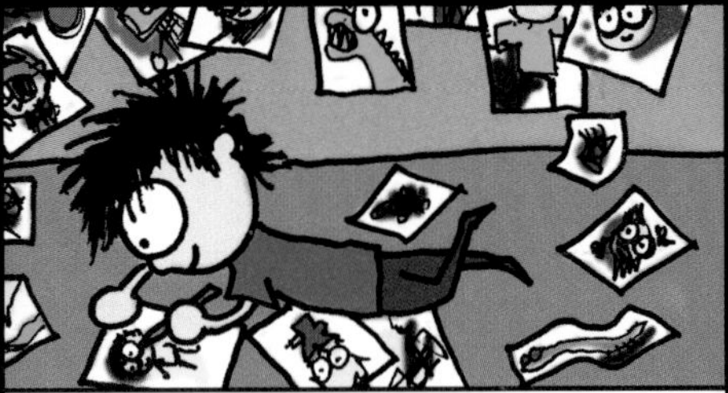

WHEN NOT HOOKED UP TO ELECTRODES, HE CAN BE FOUND IN HIS QUARTERS, MANICALLY SCRIBBLING COMICS ONTO LOLLIPOP WRAPPERS, SCRAPS OF TOILET PAPER, OR WHATEVER HE CAN GET HIS HANDS ON.

THOSE PAGES ARE COMPILED HERE AS HIS FIRST PUBLISHED BOOK, *PILOT & HUXLEY*.